Cassie couldn't hold back her laughter any longer, and she didn't complain when he dropped down next to her on the chair. As he grinned at her from much closer, she felt her breath hitch. She liked the leanness of his frame—not too built up, but not skinny. She liked that his glossy dark hair wasn't cut too short and jocky, but wasn't long and hipster-y, either. She liked the way his jeans looked like he'd actually worn them in himself rather than buying them pre-distressed. She liked that he wore his flip-flops like a good California boy, and she liked the twine necklace barely visible beneath his not-designer-but-well-fitting T-shirt.

And he was funny.

Hello, Summer Fling Number One!

"I'm Cassie," she said, extending her hand formally.

Books by Hailey Abbott:

BOY CRAZY

Hailey ABBOTT

HARPERTEEN
An Imprint of HarperCollins*Publishers*

Produced by Alloy Entertainment
151 West 26th Street, New York, NY 10001

Library of Congress catalog card number: 2009921416
ISBN: 978-0-06-125385-0

Typography by Elizabeth Dresner
09 10 11 12 13 CG/RRDH 10 9 8 7 6 5 4 3 2
❖
First Edition

Chapter One

◆

"I declare this a ten-boy summer!"

Greta Crocker's voice rang through the bedroom, distracting Cassie Morgan from the late afternoon view of the Hollywood Hills, complete with Hollywood sign. The vista over her parents' backyard and across her posh Hancock Park neighborhood reminded her that she was finally back where she belonged. Home—where Siskiyou Academy gossip, especially the Cassie-specific item involving Daniel Fletcher and her broken heart, couldn't touch her. Or shouldn't, anyway.

Enough about Daniel. Cassie fiercely tried to shake off thoughts of him as he'd shaken her off because he "needed his space." Not that she was still bitter about it. *It's summer. No ex-boyfriends or boarding school drama allowed.* She'd left all that back in her Northern California dorm on the last day of finals.

She turned her back on the view—and on her downer thoughts—to face her best friends, Greta and Keagan.

"What do ten boys have to do with our reunion summer?" Cassie made a face at her oldest friend. The Crockers had moved in next door when the girls were both four. Greta was stretched out across Cassie's four-poster bed as if it were her own—as if it had been moments rather than months since she and Cassie had laid eyes on each other. She was dressed to lounge in low-slung blue L.A.M.B. sweatpants and a clingy green Amy Tangerine T-shirt, which made her pale skin glow. Greta's strawberry-blond curls fanned out behind her as she sat up, narrowing her hazel eyes at Cassie.

"It's time to take our game to the next level before senior year starts," Greta said firmly. "Hence, ten boys."

Cassie had forgotten about Greta's bossy streak. The girls' families usually traveled during school breaks, so they hadn't actually hung out beyond very occasional coffee dates in years. E-mails and random phone calls just weren't the same as face time. But even after three years apart, they were slipping easily back into old middle school patterns.

"I was thinking more like the no-boys level," Cassie suggested, leaning back against the windowsill and smiling. "I'm ready to declare myself a boy-free zone after this last year. At least for a little while."

"Agreed." Keagan Ellison wrinkled her perfect little nose and looked up from the thick blue carpet. Cassie's second-oldest friend, whose family had moved onto the block when the girls were all six years old, had been checking out the iTunes library on Cassie's silver MacBook. She lay on her stomach, kicking her long, tanned legs up behind her. Cassie's father would have a heart attack if she tried to wear anything as short as Keagan's tiny white jean cutoffs. She loved that Keagan dared.

"I'm still recovering from the Zachary Malone disaster," Keagan said, absently pulling one of the strings on her black Ed Hardy hoodie. She shuddered dramatically, making her high, pale blond ponytail bounce. "Ugh."

Cassie had forgotten the full impact of Keagan's natural, blue-eyed prettiness, which screamed *California girl*. She ran a hand through her own darker, sandier blond mess, which she wore in a long, shaggy pixie cut. Never in a million years could she have managed to get her hair looking as smooth as Keagan's. She thought about the hated freckles that spread across her cheeks and defeated any makeup she slathered over them. She accepted with a sigh that Greta was the fashionista and Keagan the SoCal dream girl. Cassie would always look more athletic and tomboyish than her friends. Luckily, up at Siskiyou, most of the students dressed more Cassie than Keagan.

"Zachary Malone is a loser, not a disaster," Greta said, rolling her eyes. "He had asshat written all over him from day one." She looked at Cassie. "I met him once at a party. It was enough. He was vile."

"Yeah, but he's also hot." Keagan shrugged, as if she couldn't help herself. "Like, Wentworth Miller hot."

"Wentworth Miller hot is not the kind of hot you just *get over*, Greta," Cassie offered in Keagan's defense. "That's the kind of hot that requires a recovery program. Maybe even an intervention."

"I beg you," Greta said with a groan. "Don't encourage her!"

"What about you, Cassie?" Keagan asked, after sticking her tongue out at Greta. "How did your heart get broken? Vicious other woman?"

Cassie bit her tongue, feeling oddly hesitant. The three of them had been best friends before Cassie had gone off to boarding school, but their busy lives had intervened since then. Greta had had theater camps and drama club trips, and though she left long, rambling voice mails at random times, she never actually answered her phone. Keagan had joined the swim team at her school and was always traveling for meets—and even if she'd been around, she was terrible at keeping in touch. This was Cassie's first summer in Los Angeles since she'd left for Siskiyou Academy right before the ninth grade.

Cassie knew that Greta and Keagan saw *slightly* more of each other, since they still lived so close, but they went to high schools across the city from each other. They all e-mailed regularly, of course, and kept up on Facebook and stuff, but that was mostly commenting on pictures or status updates.

So how could she explain the agony and ecstasy that was Daniel Fletcher? He wasn't Wentworth Miller hot. He was . . . Daniel. He was kind of the guy equivalent of Mount Shasta, the snowcapped mountain that dominated the horizon at Siskiyou. Cassie hadn't e-mailed much about him because she didn't how to explain him. It was easier to talk to her school friends, who understood the Daniel phenomenon. He just loomed over all the other guys at Siskiyou, and Cassie had been in love with him since freshman orientation. All that wild, curly dark hair and eyes to rival the dark green woods that surrounded the school. That swagger and easy intelligence. His lazy, devastating smile. *Daniel.*

Cassie thought of the clean, crisp air and the Cascade Mountains rising on all sides, the snowy winter mornings when her boots crunched across the quad, and Daniel's warm hands against her cold cheeks on gray afternoons. After years yearning for him, she remembered what it had felt like last September when he'd smiled back at her in morning assembly. She wanted to tell her oldest friends every detail about the guy of her dreams, about curling up against him, silently breathing in the pine-scented outdoors on countless fall afternoons, about slogging through the snow to study together all winter, about getting trapped in the rain on a hike and deciding not to bother running for cover.

But it was too complicated to talk about without all of the details that made it so important, and recalling those details would lead to wallowing. Cassie didn't want to wallow. She'd been thrilled to see Greta and Keagan waiting for her when she got home the night before. And they'd seemed so excited to come over for an inaugural summer sleepover. That was what Cassie wanted to concentrate on. Her friends, not Daniel. Because, really, hadn't he caused enough pain already?

"Earth to Cassie!" Greta's voice jolted Cassie back to the present. "Where'd you go?"

"Uh-oh," Keagan replied. "Broken heart *and* a vicious other woman?"

"Daniel needed space," Cassie said with a sigh. She sank down onto the plush carpet and flexed her toes so she could see the bright pink pedicure she'd given herself peeking out from the ragged hem of her much-abused Lucky jeans. She tried to keep her voice light as if talking about it didn't still sting, and picked at a hole in the denim. "We were together all year. Then right before he left for his summer trip to Europe—with about seventeen girls, by the way—he suddenly needed space."

"Jerk!" Keagan said with feeling. She raised her brows at Greta.

"Complete jerk," Greta agreed with a frown. "Which I thought went without saying."

"Sometimes you need to say it anyway," Keagan told her, grinning. "Sometimes you even need to shout it."

"I think you guys need to seriously consider my plan," Greta pressed.

"Oh no, she has a plan!" Keagan cried with a cackle. "When has that ever ended well, Cassie?"

"Pretty much never," Cassie replied, snickering.

"I'm not talking about finding true love or any of that nonsense," Greta said impatiently. "I'm talking about *boys*. I'm talking about good old-fashioned *fun*." She eyed the other two girls. "Which it seems like both of you are in dire need of, by the way."

"What? I'm having a great summer and it's still only June," Keagan said defensively.

Greta pointed at Keagan. "There is nothing fun about sitting around, obsessing over that guy and his Heidi Montag-wannabe new chick. You know I'm right."

"Oh, please. I don't have time to obsess," Keagan argued. "I'm waiting tables at Belisimo, remember?" She made a face at Cassie. "It's this brand-new, not-at-all-Italian-even-with-that-name, way-too-snotty restaurant in

West Hollywood. But I'm hoping the tips will be worth dealing with the attitude."

"You're obsessing," Greta retorted. Keagan stuck her tongue out.

"Well, I'm always down for fun," Cassie jumped in. "It's the ten boys part that I'm not sure about. My *fun* new job starts on Saturday, anyway. What could beat leading bike tours on Catalina?"

"Riding a bike around Catalina Island all day?" Keagan asked, her eyes wide. "Every day? And I was whining about waitressing being exhausting!"

"Your sportiness fascinates me," Greta said, momentarily diverted from her ten-boys thing. "Didn't you, like, swim up and down the Mississippi River last summer or something?"

"I went on a canoe trip in the Northwest Territories in Canada." Cassie laughed. She stretched her legs out in front of her, pointing her toes until her calves complained. "On the Nahanni River, not the Mississippi. We camped in Glacier National Park. My school sponsored the trip. It was pretty amazing."

"Sporty," Greta said again, shaking her head with a smile. She rolled over on the bed and waved a hand at her willowy frame. "My idea of exercise is walking downstairs to get ice cream."

"Speaking of ice cream . . ." Cassie wiggled her eyebrows. "I believe the freezer is stocked and ready."

Laughing and whooping like they were ten years old instead of seventeen, all three girls tumbled out of Cassie's room and into the hallway, then down the polished hardwood stairs.

Jostling her way into the kitchen, with its gleaming granite counters and the huge window overlooking the spill of hot pink and cream bougainvillea in the backyard, Cassie felt the tightness that had held her hostage since Daniel started acting weird start to ease.

It had something to do with being home, to be sure. Cassie had grown to appreciate the stark shift of the seasons up near the Oregon border, but she was a Southern Cali girl at heart. She loved Los Angeles in the summer—dry and hot all day, then cool at night. She loved watching the red-and-orange sunsets over Malibu, and counting stars from the crest of the Santa Monica Mountains on Mulholland Drive. It was good to be back.

And being with Greta and Keagan again made it even better. These were the friends who'd seen her through the gawky grade-school years and would always, always be there for her—no matter how embarrassingly she'd been dumped by the most popular guy in school. Even before Daniel started to pull away, she hadn't felt this comfortable and unselfconscious in a long time.

"Tell me you have hot fudge, if you ever loved me at all!" Greta demanded as Cassie cracked open the Sub-Zero refrigerator that dominated the kitchen.

"Would I let you down?" Cassie asked, pretending to be offended, and waved the jar of hot fudge sauce in Greta's direction. Greta's joyful scream made Cassie laugh, but it also made her happy that her parents were out at some charity function.

Greta snatched the jar away from Cassie and held it against her heart, then did an exaggerated dance, as if she were auditioning for *So You Think You Can Dance with a Condiment*.

"She's nuts," Keagan said, shaking her head as she helped Cassie unload several different pints of Ben & Jerry's from the freezer. "Always has been, always will be."

"You're just jealous of me and my lover," Greta replied, still swirling and dipping around the kitchen. "My hot fudge lover."

Cassie felt a glow of happiness spread through her as the three girls arranged themselves around the center island and created an ice-cream sundae assembly line. Giggling, Cassie pulled three bowls from the cabinet and arranged them on the counter. Keagan doled out a scoop from each pint: New York Super Fudge Chunk, Coffee Heath Bar Crunch, Half-Baked, and Cassie's personal favorite, Phish Food. When the jar could be pried from Greta's hands, Cassie ladled out huge helpings of hot fudge. She and Keagan added nuts to their bowls, and all three girls threw on rainbow sprinkles. Finally, Greta squirted a giant tower of whipped cream on top of each bowl.

"Bliss," Keagan murmured, taking a big bite.

The girls padded out to the distressed-brick patio and lounged in the well-padded chairs as the sky darkened above them. The ice cream was so cold it threatened to give Cassie a sugary-sweet headache. Next to her, Greta let out a long sigh, half contented and half gluttonous. On the end, Keagan drummed her bare feet against the chair beneath her, as if keeping time with her spoon. For a while, there was only ice-cream sundae goodness, the sound of traffic far off on Melrose, and various neighborhood noises—dogs barking and the odd car stereo.

"I'm serious about this ten-boy summer," Greta said when the bowls were empty and the three of them collapsed into a lazy sprawl in the grass, holding their bellies.

"You're always serious about your schemes," Cassie replied, and smiled when Greta made a face at her. "That's why we love you."

"Listen, you two," Greta said, sitting up and crossing her legs. Her sweats dipped below her hip bones, showing a wide swath of skin underneath her green T-shirt. "You both spend way too much time stressing about unworthy guys. I say it's time to stop *worrying* about guys and start *acting* like them."

Cassie was intrigued. Keagan pulled her elastic out of her ponytail as she flipped over to her side and ran her fingers through the pale blond strands of hair that looked silvery in the dark.

"This is Greta's favorite theory," Keagan murmured. "Believe me, she will not stop talking about it. It's been like a year and a half."

"Tell me more," Cassie said.

"My philosophy is that dating like guys is the only way to have fun with the whole process," Greta explained, with a mild glare at Keagan. "Because what happens if you date like a girl? You get played like a girl. And meanwhile, he's off with the skankier clone of an MTV reality star or scampering around Europe with a posse of available women."

"Ouch," Cassie said, only half kidding. Keagan raised her eyebrows in agreement.

"So why can't we do the playing?" Greta continued. "That's the beauty of the ten-boy summer. We'll have an agreement—a quota that must be reached. You have to make it to ten, so you can't get too close to any one guy."

"What if you want to get close?" Keagan asked.

"You don't," Greta retorted. "Getting close is what made you cry in the first place. Why would you want to repeat the Zachary experience?"

Keagan made a gagging sound, but she sat up and paid closer attention.

"Exactly," Greta said triumphantly.

"So, what?" Cassie asked, frowning slightly. "We're players all of a sudden?"

"Not players," Greta said. "There's no game. This is how I operated all year. And, unlike you two, I didn't get my heart broken. And it's how guys always live their lives, by the way. What's the harm in enjoying a cute boy for exactly as long as the fun lasts and not a second longer? Not everything has to be a big relationship drama, right?"

Cassie grinned into the darkness. "Am I crazy?" she asked Keagan. "Or is she making sense?"

"I thought it was the sugar rush," Keagan replied. "But I could definitely do without any more heart stomping."

"If you don't let yourself get close," Greta said, making eye contact very deliberately with Cassie and then Keagan, "then you can't get hurt. You could spend your whole summer moping around after one guy, or you could have month's worth of fun kissing ten different ones."

Cassie bit back a giggle. "Why does this sound so appealing?"

"Because it's the wave of the future!" Greta cried. "Come on, ladies—this calls for an official pledge." She placed her right hand over her heart and held her left hand in the air. "I, Greta Crocker, do solemnly swear that I will kiss *at least* ten boys this summer, so help me God." She finished and raised her eyebrows at the other two, issuing her challenge.

Keagan laughed again. "Okay, okay," she said. "I give in." She assumed the position. "I, Keagan Ellison, do solemnly swear that I will kiss ten boys this summer and forget all about Zachary Malone, that evil loser." She shrugged. "So help me God."

"You're up, Cassie," Greta said, eyeing her. "Or are you going to sit around and *observe* all summer?"

Cassie sighed, pretending to be put out.

"I *guess* I can try to kiss some hot guys," she said, pursing her lips as if it required an internal battle. "I mean, it's gonna be a struggle."

"Poor baby," Greta teased.

"I, Cassie Morgan, do solemnly swear that I will kiss ten extremely cute boys this summer," Cassie intoned, her left hand in the air and the other tight against her chest. "I swear that I will have fun, as ordered by Greta. So help me God."

"Bring it on!" Greta cried.

"Watch out, L.A.!" Keagan called, and then collapsed into giggles.

"Let the ten-boy summer begin," Cassie pronounced, feeling the magic of summer spool out before her, drawing her in. She'd act like Greta for a change, confident and bold. She wanted Greta's take-charge attitude and her strength. Being herself had only gotten her dumped and made her mopey, neither of which had been as pleasant as kissing ten boys promised to be.

Cassie grinned. She wanted the late June night to spontaneously combust into fireworks above her to celebrate what felt like such a big shift inside her. But she was just as happy to turn to her friends instead. It was time to hash out some details.

"So," she said seriously, eyeing the other two. "Does anyone know where Robert Pattinson hangs out? Because I think we should start there."

Chapter Two

✦

Cassie was happy and relaxed that Saturday as she rode the ferry out to Catalina Island for her first day of work. Cassie loved Catalina. It was everything she adored about SoCal, all wrapped up into one gorgeous, mountainous island that rose out of the water twenty-two miles off the coast. Cassie had spent tons of weekends there throughout her childhood, hiking the interior, hanging out on the pebbled beaches, and cruising around in the golf carts that outnumbered cars in the tiny bayside town of Avalon. She'd been addicted to Big Olaf's ice cream before she knew that addiction wasn't generally a good thing, and she'd watched the fireworks over Avalon Bay on more Fourth of July nights than she could remember.

Cassie had been thrilled to cash in on her mother's longtime friendship with the owner of Billy's Bikes to hook the perfect summer job—giving bike tours in one of the most beautiful spots on earth. It certainly beat working retail in a trendy Third Street boutique like Greta, no matter how gorgeous she claimed the clothes were. And anything was better than waiting tables in too-cool West Hollywood like poor Keagan.

As she walked along the pedestrian walkway from the ferry terminal toward Avalon, Cassie soaked in the island's Mediterranean vibe. From the summer-browned hills to the sparkling Pacific water, everything about Catalina could've been out of a storybook. Even the foggy marine layer, which would burn off as the day wore on, made Cassie feel like she was part of the beauty surrounding her. After three winters way up north, the cooler morning temperatures didn't bother her the way they had when she was a thin-blooded L.A. girl. She pulled her red Siskiyou Academy hoodie tighter around her and drank in the sight of the houses and inns clinging precariously to the green and brown hillside.

It was still too early for the smell of sugar and waffle cones to fill the air outside of Big Olaf's and waft downwind as Cassie walked down Crescent Avenue, Avalon's main drag. Obvious tourists, complete with fanny packs and cameras, snapped photos of the bay and the storefronts that lined the street. Cassie smiled in anticipation of her favorite scent and turned up a side street, her steps quickening when she caught sight of the familiar sign outside of Billy's Bikes. She couldn't wait to get out on the roads and start her summer of sun, sea, and ocean breeze.

✦ ✦ ✦

MY NEW BOYFRIEND, read Greta's text a few hours later. TOTALLY WORTH GIVING UP THE OTHER 9, YES?

Cassie clicked on the attached picture, and almost choked as she half laughed, half groaned. The "boyfriend" in question was rocking the L.A. party-boy look, all battered jeans, too-tight T-shirt, and sculpted hair. But he was hot, no matter if he was Cassie's type or not.

GO 4 IT! she texted back, then slid her BlackBerry Pearl into her pocket, feeling guilty.

So far, this had turned out to be the easiest summer job in the history of summer jobs. She'd been met by a bear hug from aging hippie Billy, who had immediately sent her off for a round of morning coffee—herbal tea for him. When she'd returned, they'd gone over maps and equipment, as well as Billy's "house rules." There were only two: No "drama" and "nothing heavy before noon, because I can't process negative energy until the sun starts to descend." Which sort of both sounded like the same rule.

"That's it?" Cassie had asked, dubiously. She also wondered how her overly organized and anal mother had remained friends with this guy for so long. And whether Billy's faded, tie-dyed, Grateful Dead concert T-shirt was the real deal. "You think you should have more rules?" Billy had asked, grinning while he sipped his tea and lounged against the chipped red paint of the shop's front door. "That's intense. You're too much like your mother."

"Nothing too crazy," Cassie had said. "Just, you know, for safety reasons, I'll try not to get drunk or anything while giving tours. And to let you know if there's some big accident, so you can call a rescue team."

"Whatever works for you," Billy had told her. "As long as you're having an organic experience, I'm not going to judge you, Cassie."

Whatever *that* meant.

When noon rolled around, Billy declared it lunchtime as if they'd been slaving away all morning instead of sitting around listening to old Creedence Clearwater Revival albums at top volume. Cassie had wandered down toward the water, then over to the shops at the Metropole Hotel. She'd grabbed a sandwich before heading back toward the water, where she could daydream and stare at the sea. Talk about a perfect lunch hour!

Finally, around two, Cassie's first ever tour group was

finishing their paperwork and choosing their rental bikes. She sat on the little bench outside the shop looking down the hill toward Crescent Avenue and the sparkling bay beyond. The sun had eaten away the marine layer, and it was a glorious day. Cassie had peeled her sweatshirt off and stashed it in her backpack. She wore a snug tank top that wouldn't annoy her by flapping around when she was riding, her bike shorts, and her hiking sneakers. Her bright orange helmet was strapped to her bike, which was parked a few feet away. As soon as Billy finished with the family inside, Cassie could take them out—though not as far as she might like, since it was already midafternoon. She eyed the hills and figured she'd take the two-mile ride up to East Summit—which was a thousand feet up. Not too hard for an afternoon's ride, with acacia trees and panoramic views of the San Pedro Channel and the mainland all the way.

Her phone vibrated in her pocket, and she pulled it out, repressing the urge to look over her shoulder and see if Billy was watching her. She had to get over herself. If there was no work, why shouldn't she check her messages?

OOOH, TASTY! Keagan's text read. YOUR NEW BF USES MORE HAIR GEL THAN ALL THREE OF US PUT TOGETHER. HOTT.

U R JEALOUS, Greta had retorted, switching over to a group e-mail. HIS NAME IS JANN (YOU SAY IT YAHN) AND HE

IS EUROPEAN. HE IS IN HOLLYWOOD TO PURSUE HIS DREAM OF ACTING IN CW DRAMAS, AND HE IS DRESSING—AND HAIR GELLING—THE PART. HE'S GOING TO EAT LUNCH AT TOAST WITH SOME INDUSTRY BUDS AND GUEST STAR ON SMALLVILLE NEXT SEASON. HIS EYES TOLD ME THIS.

Cassie laughed, imagining Greta composing life stories for all of her attractive customers.

I DON'T THINK TOM WELLING NEEDS TO WORRY ABOUT HIS JOB JUST YET, she replied to the girls. NOT TO INTRUDE ON YOUR LOVE OR ANYTHING.

A few seconds later, Keagan responded: CHECK OUT THE GUYS IN MY SECTION! The attached picture was a covert shot of three guys lounging around a small table out on the sidewalk in front of Keagan's restaurant. Their menus blocked key parts of their faces, but still, the essential hotness of all three was discernible.

WAIT, Cassie replied. THEY TRAVEL IN PACKS NOW?

ONLY IN WEST HOLLYWOOD, Greta e-mailed back at warp speed. IF U KNOW WHAT I MEAN. JANN LEFT ME FOR A NASTY, TRAMPY-LOOKING CHICK WITH THE FULL HOLLYWOOD MAKEOVER—FAKE, FAKE, FAKE, Greta replied.

I THINK #1 IS MY NEW BF, Keagan e-mailed a few moments later. HIS NAME IS OBVS FREDDY AND HE'S A TOURIST FROM OHIO. HE EVEN SMELLS NICE. She attached another surveillance shot picture of "Freddy." He was round-faced, with freckles, and an adorable glint in his brown eyes.

FREDDY IS LOOKING TO HEAL A BROKEN HEART ON A SUMMER EXCHANGE PROGRAM FROM DARKEST OHIO, Cassie wrote, seized with the spirit. She jumped to her feet when the door to the bike shop opened in a jangle of chimes. Heat rushed to her cheeks.

Then she got a good look at the guy standing in front of her, surrounded by the peeling red paint that gave the shop door a speckled look. He was tall and lean, with a smooth kind of build that made Cassie think he was a runner. And he was checking her out, all the way up her legs and over her tight tank top. Cassie was suddenly thrilled that she was sporty, or whatever Greta wanted to call it, and could rock the bike shorts and the tank top. She knew she looked good. She felt a surge of Greta-style confidence, and smiled at him.

"Hey," the guy said. "Are you Cassie? We're supposed to find a Cassie." His mouth crooked up in the corner, giving him a tall, rumpled Chace Crawford look.

"That's me," she replied, smiling back. Who knew that her very first tourist would be *cute*? She'd been expecting scowling older women and tired family groups. Those had always been the people on the bike tours *she'd* taken, anyway.

"My parents said this would be a great vacation," he said, his dark eyes moving over her in obvious appreciation. "I thought they meant, you know, the beach. But we've got one of those in Boston."

"Just wait until we actually start riding," Cassie tossed back at him, trying not to giggle outright.

"I want you to know that if we get lost in the interior, I'm cool with that," he said, his grin deepening. "I'm TJ, by the way."

"Nice to meet you, TJ," Cassie replied. When his parents and two sisters came outside, TJ turned away, and Cassie whipped out her phone to snap a picture.

TJ, FLIRTY FIRST CLIENT, she typed quickly. FROM BOSTON. MAY HAVE SEVERAL GFS NAMED THINGS LIKE ELEANOR OR ASHLEY, BUT TOTALLY KISSABLE!

KISS HIM FOR ME! Greta wrote back at the speed of light. WHO CARES ABOUT GWYNETH OR AYNSLEY?

"Okay," Cassie said, stowing her phone and smiling at Summer Guy Number One, though he didn't know it yet. "Are we ready to get started?"

❖ ❖ ❖

When Cassie caught the ferry back toward Long Beach that evening, she was tired in that delicious outdoorsy way. She spent the hour-long ride catching up on the day's e-mails. She scrolled through her messages with her feet up on the hard plastic bench, her head cushioned against the side of the boat by her backpack.

Greta claimed that she had staked out Jann by walking past Toast a few times, pretending to be God only knew what, while taking pictures of Jann and his plastic girlfriend as they sat out at one of the sidewalk tables.

SHE MUST BE CASTING DIRECTOR, Greta texted at one point. ONLY EXPLANATION.

Keagan, meanwhile, had flirted up a storm with Freddy from Ohio, only to be heartbroken when he left without leaving his number—or a decent tip.

I BET HE LEFT A SWEET GIRL BACK HOME, she wrote sadly. SHE THINKS HE'S ON A SAFE FAMILY TRIP TO YOSEMITE OR SOMETHING. I FEEL SORRY FOR ME, BUT I REALLY FEEL SORRY FOR OHIOGIRL.

Cassie giggled like a fool as she read, but she didn't care if everyone on the Catalina Express stared at her. She pulled her hoodie back on and snuggled into it. Even though the sun was still out, the ferry kicked up a strong breeze as it crossed the channel.

Greta and Keagan were as delightfully silly as she remembered. She loved that they had all jumped into their ten-boy mission with both feet. Even if TJ from Boston had remained, sadly, unkissed at the end of his bike tour, Cassie felt good about giving him a few of her best smiles ever.

It occurred to her that she'd spent the entire day having fun—and not once thinking about Daniel Fletcher or his need for space. She actually laughed out loud when she realized it. There had been no wondering which of the seventeen single girls he was snuggling up to in Paris, or Munich, or Prague. In fact, this was the first time she'd even thought of his name.

Cassie sat up straight, suddenly energized, and hit "reply all."

TJ FROM BOSTON GONE—THOUGH WILL LOVE ME FOREVER, she texted. NO KISSING. BUT BIKE TOURS = HOT GUYS, APPARENTLY. WHO KNEW?

ASSUME THAT'S WHY YOU TOOK THE JOB! Greta texted back.

Amen, Cassie thought.

Daniel Fletcher could have space. He could have the entire continent of North America and the Atlantic Ocean that separated them. Cassie had everything she needed right here.

Chapter Three

✦

A week later, Cassie managed to snag a gift from the parking gods—a fantastic spot only steps from Melrose. She mouthed a quick thank-you as she locked the car and then ran around the corner and halfway down the block.

It was almost eight o'clock on the Friday before the long Fourth of July weekend, and the sun was just getting to the intensely orange part of its slide toward the ocean. Long shadows stretched across the sidewalks as dusk began to settle in. Cassie averted her gaze from one truly scary looking guy with a dark black tattoo sprawled across his forehead and a chain attached to several large piercings along his jaw. Better safe than sorry.

She pushed through the doors of her favorite coffeehouse, letting the blast of air-conditioning soothe her with the contrast from the street. The rich smell of coffee beans and warm milk enveloped her immediately, and she took a moment to breathe it in before looking around for Keagan. Her friend waved wildly from her choice spot in the plush armchairs near the window, where they could look out at all the alternative kids and gothed-out tourists who wandered in and out of the trendy boutiques, to stock up on their leathers and dog collars or grab a new tattoo before dinner.

"Sorry," Cassie said in a rush as she approached. "I got caught in traffic coming back from the ferry and then I had to change out of my bike clothes—"

"No worries," Keagan interrupted with a wave of her hand and a big smile. "I just got here myself. A toddler dumped his spaghetti all over me and it took me forever to shower it off. Seriously, it was like embedded in my hair." She made a face and waved her palms over her head, indicating the area just north of her bangs. "So gross."

"Maybe I shouldn't tell you about my day," Cassie said, collapsing into the chair opposite Keagan with a happy sigh. "The perfect all-day bike ride with the sweetest family—three generations on one trip. Grandmother, mother, and daughter." Cassie shrugged. "I had such a good time I almost missed my ferry."

"And meanwhile I was in a one-way food fight," Keagan said, wrinkling her nose. "Life is totally unfair."

"You'd never know there was a spaghetti incident," Cassie assured her, leaning back against the velvety chair. "You look great. Spaghetti- and spaghetti sauce–free."

But even covered in marinara, Keagan would have looked good. She was showing off her perfectly shaped legs in another pair of short-shorts, paired with a form-fitting red Michael Stars tank top layered under a small black vest. She'd let her hair fall around her shoulders in a pale blond curtain, and she looked like the Beach Boys might leap out at any moment and start singing about her. California cool, with a little bit of Hollywood glamour girl.

"So do you," Keagan offered. "I think I need to consume more iron or something. You're all glowing and pretty."

"I think you mean *sunburned*," Cassie laughed, though she was pleased with the compliment. She'd thrown on her favorite outfit in her rush to meet her friends—battered jeans, a bohemian-looking white peasant top that pinched in at the waist, and her most beloved dangling necklace, made of interlocking gold hoops. "If you biked in the sea air all day, you'd glow too."

"I'm so jealous that you get to be outside all day," Keagan said with a sigh. She stretched her arms over her head. "I mean, the restaurant has tables outside and stuff, but it's not really the same thing."

Cassie laughed, and then got up to order a coffee. She usually went for her favorite, Mexican mocha, which was cinnamony and chocolaty and to die for, but tonight she decided to celebrate with something *even more* decadent: a frappuccino. After all, the girls were meeting up after a long first week of working, and they were headed to their first big party together. Cassie ordered the delicious, better-than-a-milk-shake drink, and prepared herself to enjoy the sure-to-be-amazing night ahead. Not that she needed much preparation. Greta had promised the party would be overrun with hotties to suit all types. Cassie grinned at the cashier, who was all dimples and green eyes behind the counter, and there was definitely an extra spring in her step when she headed back to her armchair.

"He's cute, right?" Keagan said in a whisper, giggling. "Fully kissable, in my opinion. I'm on my second iced latte already and I blame it on his smile."

"Oh, I'll clearly be ordering another," Cassie agreed. "I wonder if he offers making out as part of the menu? Or if that's only for off-work hours?"

"I think kissing is strictly off the menu, though not necessarily off work," Keagan replied. "But I bet we could convince him." She laughed. "Just bat the eyelashes, smile, and it's practically a done deal."

"Oh, please," Cassie said, pretending to scoff. "We aren't eyelash batters. That's so submissive. We need to march up there and *demand* that he kiss us. Girl power, K!"

"My mistake," Keagan said, giggling. "No eyelashes. I'll just walk up there and when he asks if he can help me, I'll say"—she struck a pose—*"you're damn right you can. Kiss me, coffee boy."*

Cassie opened her mouth to reply, but Keagan's eyes went wide, and the color drained away from her face.

"What?" Cassie asked, worried. "You look like you've seen a ghost!"

Keagan swallowed and then let her breath out in a rush.

"Not a ghost," she muttered, splotches of color appearing on her pale cheeks. "A ghost would be okay. It's Zachary Malone. By the door."

Uh-oh, Cassie thought. Of all the eight zillion coffee shops in L.A., why did he have to pick this one?

Cassie shifted around in her seat and had no trouble picking out Zachary from the crowd. It was like he'd swaggered into some television setup crafted to make Keagan as uncomfortable as possible. Rihanna belted out a song on the sound system while the last of the day's sunshine spilled all around him in a reddish glow. He was, as expected, gorgeous. Sexy and dangerous-looking, with dark hair and one of those bodies you could tell was amazing even under a T-shirt and hipster jeans. Of course, it was also obvious that he knew he was hotter than an Abercrombie model and loved it. Wentworth Miller and then some.

And then he stepped to the side, pulling his Ray-Bans from his eyes, and revealed the girl standing next to him, clinging to his hand like she needed help to stand up straight. And she very well might have. She had fake boobs spilling out of her halter dress, big blond hair groomed to perfection, and looked way too much like Paris Hilton. Basically, she was every girl's worst nightmare.

"Yikes. . . ." Cassie managed to say.

"That's Morgana," Keagan said miserably. "Who's actually named *Morgana*?"

"Maybe it's a fake name to go with the rest of the fake body," Cassie said. Keagan only shook her head. They watched Morgana flit across the store, drawing the near-panting gaze of every guy there, until she disappeared into the ladies' room. "She's ridiculous," Cassie muttered.

"Yes, she is," Keagan replied.

Zachary glanced over and saw Keagan sitting in her chair—frozen in position like a doe in headlights. Cassie could tell the exact moment that Zachary recognized his ex. His face changed from blasé to a smirk. He took a step toward Keagan.

Oh no, Cassie thought. *This is going to get ugly.*

The door to the coffeehouse was tossed open again,

and Greta appeared in a swirl of traffic sounds with the sunset behind her, making her strawberry blond curls gleam. She was dressed to maim, in the tiniest black sundress Cassie had ever seen, with slouchy gray boots low on her legs. She strode inside the coffeehouse, smiled at Cassie, then frowned when her eyes fell on Keagan. She assessed the situation with a quick glance.

"You have to be kidding me," she said, before Zachary could say a word, her voice loud enough to reach even the screenwriters hunched over their laptops with white earbuds connecting them to their computers like life support. "Are you stalking me, *again*?" she demanded, marching right over to Zachary. "How many times can I tell you it's over?"

Greta threw a look at Cassie, eyebrows raised. Cassie took the hint and jumped to her feet as Zachary sputtered something unintelligible. Cassie followed Greta's lead.

"He just showed up," she said, even louder than Greta. She had everyone's attention. "Do you want me to call someone?"

"This is so lame," Greta said, shaking her head sadly, as if she pitied this insanely hot loser. "Why can't you stop following me around? I told you, I'm not getting back together with you, okay? It wasn't serious anyway."

"You're . . . you're crazy!" Zachary managed to get out.

"Oh, sweetie," Greta said theatrically. "I get it. I do. I'm sorry that you fell so in love with me. I wish I could feel the same."

"She wants you to leave her alone," Cassie told him, managing not to laugh—and deliberately not looking over at Keagan, who was making a suspicious wheezing sound. "She's told you a million times, Zachary. This is so embarrassing."

Zachary stared at Cassie in shock, a whole lot less hot with his mouth hanging open. Across the store, Morgana pranced out of the bathroom, oblivious to the scene taking place in front of her.

"Oh, Zach," Greta said pityingly, glancing over at Morgana. "Really? Do you *really* think that parading this poor girl around is going to make me jealous? That's almost sweet. But"—she smiled at him—"it's still not going to work, okay? I know how much you're paying her."

Zachary's face went purple, but he still couldn't seem to get a word out. From how Keagan had described him, this might be a first.

"Zach?" Morgana whined, reaching his side. "What's going on? You look super tweaked."

"Hey, buddy," said the cute cashier, leaning on the counter. "I think maybe you should leave."

"They're pretty anti-stalker here, Zachary," Cassie added, crossing her arms over her chest. "Sorry."

"And please don't leave me any more messages," Greta said, stepping around Zachary toward the counter. "I can't listen to any more of you crying, seriously. I'm sorry you're in so much pain, really I am, but you have to move on." She smiled at him. "I know I have."

And then, cool as a cucumber, Greta draped herself over the counter and ordered a double espresso, while Zachary and his new girlfriend slunk out the door. Morgana seemed confused, but if Zachary had had a tail, Cassie was certain it would have been tucked firmly between his legs. She looked over at Keagan, who was covering her mouth with both hands, her eyes wide and shining.

"Oh my God," she whispered when Cassie sank back into her seat. *"Oh my God."*

Greta walked over and perched herself on the arm of Cassie's chair, a satisfied smile on her lips.

"Greta," Keagan said, shaking her head. "I can't believe you did that! Did you see his face? Oh my *God*!"

"This is our summer," Greta said, looking at Keagan and then Cassie, and then smiling broadly. "Not his. May the games begin."

Chapter Four

✦

The first party of the summer was thrown by a kid Greta went to school with at Harvard-Westlake, one of the best private schools in Los Angeles. He lived in one of those sprawling houses in the Palisades that spread out over the bluffs with nothing to look at but the sparkling expanse of the Pacific Ocean. Cassie had always had a soft spot for the cute little village of Pacific Palisades, tucked away on Sunset Boulevard almost all the way out toward the water. It had nothing at all to do with the fact that Steven Spielberg and Tom Hanks lived in the neighborhood, she told herself as they walked up the driveway and around the ivy-covered house to the back. It had nothing to do with her secret wish that she'd be *discovered* wandering into the bookstore and suddenly find herself more famous than Miley Cyrus. Not that Cassie could act—in fact, the idea of getting up in front of a group of people and *pretending* to be something she wasn't made her blood run cold. She just enjoyed the fact that the Palisades encouraged that kind of dreaming.

Out behind the impressive house, the grassy back-yard extended to the edge of the steep bluffs, dropping off toward the Pacific Ocean far below. But it wasn't just the moonlit ocean view that made the night crackle with magic and possibility. Kids were grouped into little packs and gathered around the fire pit in the center of the grass. Others were clustered around the infinity pool. Tiki torches burned every few feet or so, marking off the edge of the property and lighting things up everywhere else. The place was jumping.

"This is already fun!" Cassie said, grinning in antici-pation.

"You know it," Greta replied. "Come on, ladies. It's time to unwind."

She led Cassie and Keagan over to the bar near the pool. Cassie followed happily, letting herself drink in all the boys that she passed. There were so many to choose from. A sweet-looking preppy guy with a knowing smile. A blond surfer god with intense blue eyes to match his board shorts. A gift bag of guys. Cassie began to think, with a little thrill inside, that it would be way too easy kissing ten of them. Why limit herself?

"Here," Keagan said, handing Cassie a beer. "You look like you're a thousand miles away. You're not thinking about the ex, are you? Because"—Keagan laughed—"the only thing an ex is good for is to allow a scene like you and Greta pulled off!"

"God, no, I'm not thinking about Daniel," Cassie said. She wrinkled up her nose. "Did you notice that this place is crawling with kissable boys?"

"That's the right attitude," Greta chimed in. She leaned in close and clanked her beer bottle against the other two. "This party is filled with worthy candidates."

They all toasted and took big gulps of their drinks.

Then Cassie and Greta stared as Keagan chugged the remainder of her beer, tossed it into one of the garbage pails nearby, and swiped herself a new one from the nearby cooler. She took the first sip from her new bottle and then raised her eyebrows at her friends.

"What?" she asked. "I've had a long night."

"Candidates," Cassie said, changing the subject in a hurry. She didn't know what *she* would have done if it had been Daniel who'd sneaked up on her like that. "I like that term. All these cute boys are just *candidates* waiting to be chosen. *Maybe*. If they pass my grading system."

"You have a grading system?" Greta asked, arching an eyebrow.

"Well, no," Cassie admitted. "But I think I should."

"Me too," Keagan said, shrugging her shoulders as if warding off a shiver. "I'm going to do a lap and see what there is to see." She gave a wicked sort of smile. "Don't worry if you see me talking to strangers, okay?"

Greta laughed slightly as Keagan sauntered off, working those short-shorts with every step, her long, pale hair waving behind her like a veil.

"She cracks me up," Greta said. "I love it when she gets in touch with her dark side."

"Does she not usually?" Cassie asked. She genuinely didn't know what her friends were like when she wasn't around. It made her sad to think about how much life they all lived without one another. This summer was her chance to finally see it all, rather than hearing summaries and stories in past tense.

"She's got that whole innocent vibe thing working for her," Greta said. She looked at Cassie. "You know. She looks like a delicate little angel, and that's how guys usually treat her. Or want to see her, anyway."

"She's not an angel tonight," Cassie murmured, indicating Keagan with her drink. "Check it out."

Greta turned, and both of them watched as Keagan flirted with a brawny football-player type, with massive shoulders and dark hair. Keagan was already showing her dimples and moving closer.

"She doesn't waste any time," Greta said with a laugh. "Go, Keagan!" She made a face and cast an eye around the party. "Unfortunately, I go to school with a lot of these people, so I am less excited with the potential than you are." She shrugged at Cassie's look. "I've either already kissed or decided not to kiss most of the guys here. But there's no reason you can't start working on *your* numbers."

Cassie took another swig of her beer and met the challenge in Greta's gaze with a smile.

Flirting and introducing herself to new guys was seriously exciting. She and Greta worked as a team, insinuating themselves into groups, having teasing conversations with the boys, and then moving on. Cassie followed Greta's lead. She'd never felt so confident before. It was like something that bubbled beneath her skin, making her giddy. Was this how it felt to be Greta?

On her way to get a second beer, Cassie looked over toward the last place she'd seen Keagan—and stopped short.

"Whoa!" Greta cried, bumping into her from behind.

"Um, look over there," Cassie said, waving across the pool deck. Greta turned.

They both stood frozen still for a moment, taking in the view of Keagan completely making out with Mr. Football Shoulders. And, if her swaying body was any indication, she was also wasted.

"Huh," Greta said after a moment. "I did not see Keagan being first out of the gate on this. An unexpected twist." Her voice sounded impressed. Proud, even.

"Maybe, you know, this is healing," Cassie said philosophically, while across the way Keagan lost her balance and tipped against the guy holding her up. "It's probably a good thing for her, to help her over her ex, once and for all."

"And nothing helps a broken heart like making out with a total stranger," Greta said with a happy sigh. "When's the last time you did something like that?"

Cassie considered. "There was no broken heart," she said after a moment, "but I did make out with this hot skateboarder guy last summer. He was at one of the campgrounds, and there was a bonfire, and . . ." She shrugged, grinning. "Then there were lips."

"You hussy!" Greta pretended to be scandalized. "Do you even know his name?"

"It had to be Wade or something," Cassie said, frowning.

"Wade?" Greta cackled. "*Wade* is the go-to name?"

"It was weird, but not too weird!" Cassie protested. "What about you?" She laughed. "Wait a minute, I forgot who I was talking to."

"Yes, Cassie," Greta said, grinning, her hand propped on her hip. "I have made out with strange boys. It's the fun new way to say hello. You should see if there are any more *Wades* hanging around this party." She pointed at a set of deck chairs, where a mixed group of girls and guys was sitting. "I'm going to head over there. Grab us some drinks and come join us."

Cassie decided to pace herself, and snagged herself a Coke with Greta's next beer. Then she made her way through the groups of kids. The jasmine-scented summer night lay heavy all around them. The Killers were blaring from the speakers, and she could feel the thump of the bass in her bones. A group of girls was dancing together on the grass, laughing wildly. Cigarette smoke rose in a cloud from a pack of guys sitting around the fire pit. She could smell salt and brine from the ocean, and the scent made her smile.

Cassie excused herself when she bumped into a couple who were a little too tied up with each other, then nimbly danced around them. She picked her way through the group Greta had joined and took the seat Greta had saved next to her.

"Everyone, this is Cassie," Greta announced. "She lives next door to me." She looked at Cassie. "These people all go to my school."

There was a chorus of "Hi, Cassie," from the group, and more than one "Why haven't we met you before?"

"I go to boarding school," Cassie said. "Siskiyou Academy, up north of Redding."

"Ugh, cold," groaned a girl who looked like a stereo-typical Orange County surfer chick. "I'm Jessica, and anything below seventy degrees and I have, like, hypo-thermia."

Cassie grinned a hello.

"I would love to go to boarding school," another guy chimed in. "How cool would that be? No parents."

"Clayton is always grounded," Greta said. "Also, this is his house." She made a face at Clayton. "Do you think maybe the fact you throw huge parties might have some-thing to do with getting grounded?"

"My parents shouldn't go on trips if they don't want me to have parties," Clayton retorted. He returned his attention to Cassie. "Boarding school would be the answer to my prayers."

"I guess," Cassie agreed. "But there are teachers. Though this one—"

"Oh no," Greta interrupted. Cassie's story died on her lips. She stared at Greta, wondering what she'd done—but Greta's attention was focused on Keagan.

Keagan was drunkenly leaning on the arm of her kissing buddy as he headed toward the gate. Cassie frowned at the spectacle. Her friend was giggling uncontrollably, and it didn't look like she could walk on her own.

"Is he taking her home?" Cassie asked.

"Um, over my dead body," Greta retorted, standing

up. "I don't know that guy." She started walking toward Keagan, her strides purposeful in her slouchy boots. "Hey! K! Wait up!" she called.

Cassie couldn't help smiling as she watched Greta take charge. First she disentangled Keagan from Mr. Football Shoulders. Then she shooed him away, without appearing to notice his complaints. And then she towed Keagan over to a group of girls she knew, and started negotiating a ride for Keagan from one of them. Cassie was still smiling when Greta, holding Keagan up, disappeared around the side of the house.

That was Greta. Bossy sometimes, yes. But as she'd proved twice tonight, she could always be counted on in a crisis.

Cassie returned her attention to the group around her. They'd reshuffled while the Keagan drama unfolded. Clayton had wandered off to a different clump of people, while Jessica was whispering to a girl who looked like she'd gotten dressed from the same closet. Cassie found she had an entire lounge chair to herself. So she did what any free, single, and happy girl would do—she lay back in it like she ruled the party. She closed her eyes, smiled, and soaked in her surroundings, memorizing everything from the sound of Kanye on the speakers to the laughter of the guys on the lounge chair next to her, and the ocean air embracing them all.

"Excuse me, Your Majesty," came a drawling voice from above, a voice that sent a delicious shiver down Cassie's spine. "May I share your throne?"

Cassie opened her eyes, and her perfect summer night got a whole lot better.

Chapter Five

◆

The guy looking down at Cassie made her mouth go dry. He had dark eyes, darker hair, and the sexiest smile Cassie had ever seen in real life. Her heart kicked into high gear, and she could feel her blood pound through her veins. He stood over her, grinning, and practically oozing confidence. She felt light-headed.

"May I?" He gestured toward her chair.

"I don't know," she replied, trying to casually rub away the goose bumps that snaked down her arms. She kept it light. "What makes you think you deserve to share my throne?"

"I'm excellent at sharing," he replied, laughter in his gaze. "It's been the case since preschool, just so you know. I'm a lifelong good sharer."

"You must be so proud of your record," Cassie teased him. She eased herself up to a sitting position, aware that his eyes stayed on her as she moved. "Can you claim the Southern California title?"

He blew out a breath, considering. "I don't mean to sound conceited," he said seriously, though his dark eyes danced. "But I'm the state champion. And the western division champion, as a matter of fact. There's a good sharer from Philadelphia who might throw me some competition in a national tournament, but I'm not worried. We can both have the title. See? Sharing is in my blood."

Cassie couldn't hold back her laughter any longer, and she didn't complain when he dropped down next to her on the chair. As he grinned at her from much closer, she felt her breath hitch. She liked the leanness of his frame—not too built up, but not skinny. She liked that his glossy dark hair wasn't cut too short and jocky, but wasn't long and hipster-y, either. She liked the way his jeans looked like he'd actually worn them in himself rather than buying them pre-distressed. She liked that he wore his flip-flops like a good California boy, and she liked the twine necklace barely visible beneath his not-designer-but-well-fitting T-shirt.

And he was funny.

Hello, Summer Fling Number One!

"I'm Cassie," she said, extending her hand formally.

"Queen Cassie," he said in an overly polite tone. When he gripped her palm with his, Cassie felt dizzy. "I'm Trey." He let go of her hand, but Cassie could still feel the press of his warm skin against hers. "I haven't seen you around before," he continued. "You definitely do not go to Harvard-Westlake like the rest of these people. I would have noticed."

"We queens like to maintain our mystique," Cassie told him. He laughed.

"I can see that." He flicked his gaze over her, taking in the knees she'd pulled up under her and the swath of skin she knew her shirt had pulled up to expose at her waist. She didn't make a move to pull her shirt back into place. Instead, Cassie felt warm and bold. She liked him looking at her.

"What do you do when you're not queen of all you survey?" he asked.

"Lead bike tours out on Catalina," Cassie told him, dropping the royal act. "I work for Billy's Bikes. Today I took three generations of one family out on a tour—a grandmother, her daughter, and *her* daughter. They were completely into it. It was so cool."

"That's like the perfect summer job," Trey said, leaning back on his hands. "I love Catalina."

"Me too," Cassie said, pleased. He really was good at sharing. "I haven't spent the summer in L.A. since starting boarding school, but how could I pass up a job like that?"

"Seriously," Trey said. "A few summers ago I took this awesome bike trip in Maine with my dad and a few of my cousins. One hundred and forty miles through Acadia National Park and along the coast. It was the best."

"I've never been out East," Cassie said with a sigh. "Maine is supposed to be beautiful. Especially in the summertime."

"It's great," Trey said. He smiled. "But it's not Catalina."

"Someday you'll have to come out and see Catalina through my eyes," Cassie said, feeling courageous and cool. She thought she could have given Greta, resident flirting expert, a run for her money. "I hear I'm a terrific tour guide."

"I believe it," Trey said, his voice warm.

"What about you?" she asked, feeling dazzled.

"My parents weren't about to let me lie around the house for my last summer before college," Trey said, shifting on the chair so that his legs were tantalizingly close to Cassie's. "So I have to rearrange my dad's entire filing system—which kind of sucks because he's a lawyer and has, like, eight million files—but I can't really complain. I can set my own hours and do my own thing."

"Are you nervous about college?" Cassie asked.

"Nervous?" He shrugged. "Were you nervous about boarding school when you went?"

"Totally!" Cassie shuddered, making him laugh. "I

thought I was going to pass out the day I left. I'd lied to all my friends about how thrilled I was to go to Siskiyou and then I actually had to go *do* it." She wrinkled her nose. "I was a mess."

"I don't know," Trey said. "I'm kind of looking forward to everything being new." He laughed again. "Although I don't know how new it's really going to be. My parents met at Stanford, and I've been hearing about the place my whole life."

"New for you is still new," Cassie said, smiling at him. "And new is good."

"Yes," Trey said, holding her gaze for a long moment. "It definitely is."

Some girls shrieked with laughter nearby, shattering the moment, and Cassie felt heat creep across her cheeks when she looked away from him. It was like she was waking up from a spell. And he was still watching her when she looked back, which made everything worse. Or better.

Trey's mouth curved a little bit. His gaze felt like heat against Cassie's skin. "Don't go anywhere," he said. "I want to get you a drink, and then I want to hear more about you."

"Get me a Coke, and I'll tell you," Cassie said with another of the flirty smiles that seemed to be coming to her so naturally to her tonight.

Trey's grin widened, and then he pulled himself to his

feet and headed for the coolers near the bar. Cassie watched him walk away, admiring the way he moved, low and easy. He had to be an athlete. He walked with that kind of confidence, and he stood out from the rest of the guys at the party. He looked a little too tall for soccer, and too lean for football, unless he was the quarterback. Maybe lacrosse? She'd have to ask him when he returned.

And she knew he'd return. She could *feel* it. How could a guy so cute be that easy to talk to? It was like a fantasy, to go along with the Palisades house and the sweet night air. In her experience, boys as cute as Trey were totally conceited once they started talking. Cassie watched Clayton slap him on the back and both of them laughed. Trey seemed to be a bright light while everyone else was on a dimmer and faded next to him.

"Damn." Greta's voice came from behind Cassie, startling her. "It's one drama after another tonight."

"Where did you come from?" Cassie asked, turning to look into Greta's hazel eyes. "How's Keagan doing?"

"She's on her way home," Greta said. "Hopefully not passing out in Jennifer Wilhelm's father's Lexus SUV." She sat down next to Cassie, her face way too serious for Cassie's giddy mood.

"Is she okay?" Cassie asked, suddenly worried that while she'd been trying to kiss Summer Boy Number One, Keagan might have been in real trouble. What kind of friend did that make her? Apparently, the kind of friend who also kind of wished Greta hadn't sat there—because where would Trey sit when he came back? *You're terrible,* she scolded herself.

"She's fine," Greta said. She searched Cassie's face for a long moment, as Cassie's agitation grew. "What were you doing with Trey Carter?"

"Oh," Cassie said, laughing slightly. Her cheeks flushed. "Do you know him? Greta, seriously, he's the most—"

"He's a player," Greta interrupted flatly.

"What?" Cassie blinked. "No, I don't think so. No way." And she also wondered where Greta got off calling anyone a player, given her philosophy on boys and the way they should be treated as disposable amusements.

"Trust me, he is." Greta shook her head and crossed her arms over her chest. "He was like the biggest dog in his graduating class. He uses girls and tosses them aside like Kleenex. I watched him over here with you and believe me, I've seen it before. I'm sorry, but I have."

"But . . ." Cassie couldn't believe what she was hearing. "We were just having some fun, Greta. I don't think—"

"Trey Carter is not about having fun," Greta said, in that same matter-of-fact tone. "Trey Carter gets off on messing with girls' feelings. He likes to humiliate them. It makes him feel powerful or something."

Cassie's mouth hung open. "But he was so funny and easy to talk to!"

"That's how he does it," Greta said grimly. "I love you, Cassie, and I don't want to see you get hurt." She reached over and put her hand on Cassie's leg. Her gaze was clear and direct. "You need to stay away from him."

Cassie couldn't seem to hold on to a complete thought. She'd been buzzing with excitement—and now she felt heavy and embarrassed. But how could Greta be right? Wouldn't she have gotten a sleazy vibe from Trey? Instead of that thrilled, magical feeling?

She turned her head and scanned the crowd for him. She wanted to look up and see Trey hurrying back. Not that that would prove anything, necessarily. But instead, when she spotted him, he was standing at the drinks table.

Surrounded by about ten girls.

It was exactly like that horrible vision she tortured herself with, except the vision was usually Daniel Fletcher and his seventeen European bimbos. Trey and a bevy of girls was a new twist, but really, so very much the same old thing. Cassie winced. It turned out new wasn't always so good after all.

"I'm such an idiot," Cassie muttered, looking away from Trey and his girls. She forced herself to smile. "And I didn't even get a kiss out of it."

"Everybody falls for his act," Greta said, her voice

moving from flat to something more sympathetic. "You can't beat yourself up about it."

But Cassie was furious with herself. This was why she'd agreed to the ten-boy summer in the first place. She was supposed to be focused on racking up the kisses, not serious romance. She obviously couldn't rely on her own intuition. She would have happily let Trey play her—all because she was a sucker for a guy who showed earnest interest in things she cared about.

But no more. No more trying to get close. No more letting herself fall for guys, no matter how delicious it felt. No more.

"Hey," she said, nudging Greta with her shoulder. "You know what would hit the spot right now?"

"A little Trey Carter bashing?" Greta asked wryly. "I could be into that."

"Cheese fries," Cassie said. She wanted to be over Trey Carter and his womanizing ways. "Gooey, hot, and in all ways bad for us comfort food."

Greta grinned. "The only thing better than Trey Carter bashing," she said with a laugh. "Let's go."

Cassie stood without a backward glance.

She told herself she didn't even want to look to see if Trey noticed.

But not turning around was the hardest thing she'd done all summer.

Chapter Six

◆

The morning after the party Cassie's alarm went off way too early. Nothing about getting up at 6 a.m. was okay—even if she'd gone to bed at eight the night before, which she definitely hadn't. Cassie moaned, bleary-eyed, and staggered into the shower. She didn't really wake up until she was halfway down the freeway toward her 8:30 a.m. ferry, sucking down the cold-brewed coffee she'd brought with her from home.

Sweet, sweet caffeine. The only thing that made the long commute bearable. That and the fact that she didn't really have to appear bright-eyed or bushy-tailed until she arrived at the bike shop—which was another hour ahead of her. Cassie had figured that her ferry ride would provide a much-needed extra hour of rest on difficult mornings. And this was definitely a difficult morning.

Cassie parked and made her way onto the ferry, settling into her favorite seat up top. It was windier outside and sometimes got a little cold so early in the morning, but she hated being cooped up inside the boat's cabin. She liked to see the sunlight bounce off the waves as it gained strength. She liked to ride the swells and see the California mainland get smaller in the distance, so that even the great sprawl of Los Angeles began to look manageable.

The ferry finally got under way, and Cassie relaxed as the engine thrummed beneath her. She stared off at the water in front of her and wondered what the day would hold. She knew she should probably eat something for energy, but she was still full from last night's Denny's stop with Greta. They'd gone to town on the cheese fries, and while Cassie didn't regret a single bite, she'd had no appetite at all for her usual eaten-while-commuting bagel. Luckily, she always carried a few Luna bars in her backpack for inevitable moments of starvation on a tour.

Cassie let the morning wash over her—fresh sea air and the salt sting—and was feeling pretty great about life in general when she noticed a guy leaning against the rail a little ways away from her, closer to the bow of the boat.

He was propped up on his elbows and staring out at the water, and she could only see his back, but for a second—

She must still have Trey Carter on the brain, she thought, shaking her head, because the guy looked a lot like she imagined Trey would look—if he were wearing Abercrombie khaki shorts and a dark red sweatshirt, that is, and if he were randomly on her ferry. She was still annoyed at herself for failing to pick up on the fact that Trey was a loser. The farther away she got from that lounge chair in Pacific Palisades, the more she regretted letting Trey get into her head. The fun of all the flirting she and Greta had done, the sweet summer evening, the excitement of their first big party in a long time—all of this had obviously confused her senses and foiled her jerk radar.

What if Greta hadn't been looking out for her? Cassie pulled her hoodie tighter around her and tried to burrow into it. It didn't bear thinking about.

She wasn't prepared when the guy at the rail turned and showed his face. Cassie was astounded to discover he didn't just look like Trey Carter.

He *was* Trey Carter.

Cassie's mouth fell open in shock. Trey walked over and sat next to her as if it were still the night before and she'd been keeping the spot open for him. Cassie was far too flabbergasted to react in time.

"I woke up this morning seized with this *need* to go to Catalina," he said casually, as if they were still in the same conversation they'd been in the night before. As if nothing had changed. "What do you think that's about?"

"Um, I have no idea," Cassie muttered, not looking at him. She looked at her feet, which usually seemed ungainly to her, but somehow looked cute next to Trey's much bigger ones. Okay—not helpful. "Catalina is a very popular destination."

"I have a theory," Trey confided in a low voice. The kind of voice that invited Cassie to lean in so that she could hear every word. She wanted to. But she reminded herself that this was undoubtedly one of his many games. It was horrifying how much she wanted to be played in that moment—it was like some physical weakness in her bones—but Cassie decided that was simply because he was so talented. It wasn't *her* weakness, it was *his* skills.

"I don't think you need a theory," she said, trying to sound bored and over him. "It's Catalina in the summer. It's self-explanatory."

If Greta had said that, Cassie knew, it would have been cutting and decisive. It would have sliced into Trey and sent him scuttling off to lick his wounds. But she knew it hadn't sounded that way coming out of her mouth. Even if he'd picked up the sarcastic tone of her voice, Trey showed no signs of scuttling. Instead, he looked straight at her, his dark eyes knowing and a little curve in the corner of his mouth.

"My theory is about a girl," he said in that same low, inviting way. Damn him. He totally ignored her attempted rebuff and picked up where he'd left off. Smooth. "My theory is that she deliberately bailed on me at a party without so much as giving me a phone number, leaving me no choice." He grinned. "Normally I might text or something, but with no number? A trip to Catalina was the only way."

Cassie tried to think about the situation objectively. And objectively, she could see that Trey was distractingly sexy. Objectively, she would have found this moment adorable and romantic had Greta not told her his real motives. It was almost sad that she knew he was playing games, because otherwise she would have melted into a puddle on the deck of the *Catalina Express*. A less-prepared girl wouldn't have stood a chance. The guy was good.

"I admit that I'm not used to being blown off," Trey said when she didn't respond. "But you warned me that you were mysterious."

"And you like that?" Cassie asked. She already knew he liked it. Greta had told her that when he set his sights on someone, he was entirely dedicated to the pursuit. *Chase and destroy.*

"I like mysteries I can solve eventually," Trey said. His smile encouraged her to smile in return. "I think it comes from reading too much Christopher Pike when I was a kid."

Cassie's eyes lit up despite herself. "I loved Christopher Pike!" she cried. "I lived for the Spooksville books."

"Me too," Trey said. "I used to read them under my covers with a flashlight when I was supposed to be asleep."

What was she *doing*?

"Excuse me," Cassie announced abruptly, with unnecessary formality. Because what else could she do? Looking at him wasn't doing any good—the red Stanford sweatshirt was practically mesmerizing her at this point, managing to look cozy even as it clung to his well-formed chest. That was the only explanation for her sudden desire to talk about favorite childhood books with him. So she quickly got to her feet and went inside, where she stood on line to use the restroom even though all she did once there was glare at herself in the mirror. *Christopher Pike? Really?* Then she bought a coffee and went out to the other side of the boat. She wouldn't have to worry about Trey's tactics if she wasn't anywhere near him, would she?

Cassie managed to avoid him the rest of the way across the water, but her luck ran out when they docked at Avalon. She'd barely disembarked when Trey fell into step beside her.

"Another beautiful California morning," he said, sounding perfectly happy, as if she hadn't run out in the middle of another conversation. Maybe he wasn't so much a player as he was just crazy.

She tried to walk faster, but it was a wasted effort. Trey easily kept pace with her, and before she knew it they were walking into Billy's Bikes together. She figured that would end things pretty quickly. Surely he didn't want to hang out in a bike shop all day.

Especially *this* bike shop. Billy celebrated their arrival by turning up the music to deafening levels and racing out from behind the counter to rock back and forth to the pounding drums.

"Terrapin Station!" he shouted above the music, curving his hands into what he had told Cassie was a particular Deadhead dance. He looked as if he were cradling a giant yet invisible ball in his arms and rocking it back and forth in midair.

Cassie brushed past Billy and turned the stereo down.

"I think the windows are about to shatter," she told him. She pretended Trey wasn't there. This was not an unusual way for perpetually tie-dyed Billy to begin the workday. Cassie was used to it by now. But that didn't mean it wasn't loony.

She was completely surprised when Trey signed up for her bike tour.

"What are you doing?" she hissed at him, after he'd handed over his money and been swept away from the counter by a pack of noisy tourists who claimed Billy's attention.

"What does it look like I'm doing?" he asked, tilting his head slightly as he looked down at her, like she wasn't making sense.

"Why would you want to go on a bike tour?" she asked, exasperated. "You've been to Catalina a million times."

"Is this the same Cassie who told me I had to see the island through her eyes?" Trey asked lightly. "And since when is a bike ride in paradise not worth doing?"

Cassie was fuming, but she couldn't do anything about it. She had to help get the bikes ready for the tour group and pack up her emergency kit. Billy, naturally, was engrossed in a conversation with a similarly hippied-out Catalina native about "Dark Star," which Cassie now knew was a particular Grateful Dead song. She managed to completely ignore Trey until she'd gathered the day's tour group in front of her and was giving her usual welcome speech.

She nearly forgot her well-practiced words halfway through, because he was just *watching* her. Like he was trying to figure her out.

"I have extra water and a first-aid kit," she finished. "Don't be afraid to ask for either one if you need it!"

"Don't worry about this group," the middle-aged woman nearest Cassie said with a laugh, fastening her helmet to her head. Cassie had to concentrate to remember her name, but it finally came to her: Felicia. "We are not afraid to sing out if we need something!"

The whole group burst into laughter at that one.

"I take it you all know each other," Cassie said dryly. Cue more laughter.

"The eight of us go on a vacation together every year for the Fourth of July," Felicia said, reminding Cassie that the holiday was on Monday. "We girls have all been friends since college."

"While we husbands have learned to get along with each other one way or another," one of the men joked. Cassie laughed along with them, wishing Trey would go away.

But he not only wasn't going anywhere, he was actually helping the tourists as they started on the ride. He taught three of them the proper hand signals and had two of the men in stitches as he told a story about his bike trip in Maine. Cassie was torn between amazement at the effectiveness of his spell, even on adults, and jealousy that he'd gone to all the trouble to take her bike tour and now wasn't paying any attention to her. What was wrong with her?

"Your boyfriend is a hoot!" Felicia called over to Cassie as they started the climb into the hills.

"He's not my boyfriend!" Cassie called back, and then felt her cheeks heat when Felicia gave her an assessing look.

Happily, the steep hill ahead of them took care of any more boyfriend talk.

Cassie tried to block Trey out and focus on the beautiful summer morning all around her. The sun and the sea and the island's hills were all that mattered. Not some loser who apparently had to be the most popular guy around, even with a group of old, married tourists.

Trey pulled ahead of the group, his bike surging forward under his sure hands and strong legs, and charged up the incline. Cassie couldn't help but admire the way he handled himself. He spun around in a circle, letting out a whoop, and then coasted back down toward the tour group. His smile was wide and his face was filled with the same fierce joy Cassie felt every time she took this ride. Her chest tightened as she looked at him. She had to concentrate to get her breath back.

She tried to shake it off when they made their first stop. Everyone gratefully took the little snack packs she handed out, and complimented her on the first leg of the tour as if she had anything to do with the island's beauty. Cassie made sure not to look too much at Trey, who had stripped his sweatshirt off and was looking far too delicious in his white T-shirt. It was dangerous enough that he was so gorgeous, but what she felt suddenly was a lot more tender. It confused her.

"Trey," Felicia said then, in her commanding voice

that could probably be heard back in Avalon, "Cassie tells me you're not her boyfriend."

Cassie died in that moment. Or, at least, she wished she had. The rest of Felicia's friends laughed, but Cassie's ears were ringing and she could feel all the blood in her entire body race to her face.

She was still alive. Unfortunately.

"No, ma'am," Trey said, sounding far too amused.

"Life is short," Felicia announced. "You should take her out sometime. Do kids date these days? Or *hang out*, as my daughter claims?"

"I think it's *hanging out*," one of her friends said. "*Dating* is so old-fashioned."

Trey looked over at Cassie, a tiny crook of a smile flirting with his mouth—and wreaking havoc with Cassie's nervous system. Which she figured made her twice the fool. She knew all about him and he still got under her skin.

"I don't think Trey needs anyone's help, but thanks," Cassie said, humiliated that her voice was so squeaky. "And actually, I'm, uh, totally good as is. So. Who's ready for the next leg?"

She made a big show of fussing over her bike and collecting trash, but she could feel Trey's eyes on her the whole time. She refused to look back and confirm.

She told herself she started shivering because the wind picked up, but she knew she was lying. For the rest of the ride, she kept her mouth shut and led the group silently. Trey didn't try to talk to her again, but she felt him watching her all the way down the trail. By the time they got back to the bike shop, she had to fight back the truth—she loved that he was looking.

Chapter Seven

✦

With the Fourth of July behind them, the three girls decided that the following Saturday night was time to take what Greta had dubbed Project Kiss to the next level: clubbing.

"Enough with boys we've already dated, or go to school with, or have, like, *met* already," Greta had declared earlier in the week. They'd been relaxing after work at Keagan's parents' house, enjoying the hot tub.

"Seriously," Keagan had agreed. "Something different is definitely in order."

"I want to hit a club this weekend," Greta had continued.

"Yes!" Cassie had cried. It had been far too long since

she'd gone out dancing. "New and undiscovered boys! Bring it on!"

Which was how the three of them had ended up in skimpy outfits and high heels outside Club Danger on Cahuenga Boulevard. When Cassie was a kid, she'd spent her Sunday mornings in this very same neighborhood with her parents. Every Sunday was the Hollywood Farmers' Market, which took over the streets, barring all cars and making the area a pedestrian walkway. The streets were crowded with white-canopied tents and the smell of earth and fresh produce. People wandered around with bulging baskets, munching on perfectly ripened tomatoes or sweet berries. Cassie and her father would always pick up fresh tamales from the tamale truck and eat them while they walked, while Cassie's mom gathered fresh-caught fish and heavenly smelling loaves of bread baked that morning.

It was exciting to see how much the neighborhood had changed. It was now home to all kinds of hot new clubs and bars. Someone was obviously trying to make the most of what had once been a super-seedy neighborhood boasting not much more than the Arclight, Cassie's favorite movie theater in the world. But the fact that the neighborhood had become cool while Cassie wasn't paying attention didn't make up for the fact that her feet hurt and standing in line was boring. Plus, she suspected that the bouncer was only making them all wait so that people would think the club was über-exclusive—because they'd been in line a while and no one had gone near the door.

"I hate waiting," Cassie muttered, shifting her weight from one foot to the other. She'd borrowed one of Greta's crazy-short dresses, and was trying to appreciate how long her legs looked rather than think about how much of her upper thighs were on display. Her outfit was far outside her comfort zone. She wore a shiny gold micromini dress that clung to her body and ridiculously high platform sandals with crisscrossing straps that made her feet ache. Keagan had applied Cassie's makeup, using a lot more eye shadow than Cassie would have, and had also done Cassie's hair so that it looked like she'd spent all day at a magical beach that didn't ruin perfectly tousled waves. Greta had approved. She'd called Cassie "messily hot."

Cassie wanted to feel hot. Instead, she felt self-conscious. She realized she was tugging the tiny dress farther down her legs and forced herself to stop.

"You need to learn how to live in the moment," Greta murmured back, her voice all vampy. She was also wearing a micro dress in her signature black, but with bright red ankle boots. "There's a lot of eye candy right here, and no one's pushing you to get to the bar."

Keagan and Cassie exchanged a look and giggled as

Greta pointed out a guy a little ways in front of them in the line snaking down the sidewalk. He smiled at Greta's obvious point, and Cassie thought that maybe he was a little too Hollywood for *her*—gelled hair, carefully constructed outfit—but maybe he was perfect for Greta.

"See?" Greta asked. She turned back to her friends. "Where are we on Project Kiss, anyway? It's already the second week of July. Time's running out."

"I'm good," Keagan said brightly. She started ticking off kisses on her fingers. "There was the football guy from that party in the Palisades, obviously. And some random guy at a soccer cookout I went to the next day. And then that cutie with the sideburns and the guitar at the barbecue on the Fourth."

"You missed a great barbecue, Cassie," Greta said.

"Don't rub it in," Cassie moaned. "I've missed the family reunion for the past three years. My parents insisted I go this summer." It had been nice to see all of her relatives and hang out in the hills near San Diego, but Cassie would have much preferred to spend the holiday with her friends.

"It was at a funky house in West Adams," Greta said. Her hazel eyes sparkled. "I kissed one of the guys in the band, and then later made out with this other guy who claimed he was the band manager. I think he was making that up, but who cares? He was yummy."

"You guys are killing me!" Cassie complained. "I

talked to my grandmother. My uncle Bobby quizzed me about my future plans. Ugh."

"That's why we're here," Keagan said in a soothing tone. "You can totally kiss your way around the club."

"All I've had so far was the near miss with TJ from Boston," Cassie said, pretending to hang her head in shame. "I'm a disappointment to us all."

"Don't forget your close call with Trey Carter," Greta said with a snort. "That could have been a much bigger disaster."

"Luckily, you saved me," Cassie said lightly. She felt a pang of guilt. She should have told her friends about Trey's unexpected appearance on Catalina the day after the party, but she hadn't. She didn't know why she'd kept it to herself, and a whole week had gone by. How could she bring it up now?

And then, as if in answer to her prayers, the line began to move.

"What are you smiling about?" Keagan asked, looking especially mysterious with lots of dark mascara and a high, sassy ponytail. Her dress was slightly longer than Cassie's but made up for it by plunging to nearly her navel.

"This is going to be a great night," Cassie told her, slinging one arm over her shoulders. She shoved Trey Carter out of her head and moved toward the sound pounding out from the club. "I can just tell."

Inside, Greta immediately peeled off with her eye candy, who'd been waiting for her just inside the doors, near the coat check.

"Don't do anything I wouldn't do!" Greta sing-songed. Cassie watched Greta saunter toward the guy, swinging her hips. She almost blended in with the black walls that made the entrance to the club feel like a cave. Dance music filled the air and shook the walls. People streamed past them, some headed into the main club area to the left, others straight ahead toward the bath-rooms.

"That was quick," Keagan said with a laugh, pulling Cassie forward, away from the entryway and farther into the club. "His friends are checking us out, if you're inter-ested."

Cassie shot a look over her shoulder, then shrugged. Three guys returned her look, all of them dressed in that super-stylized Hollywood way. They were good-looking, but they looked like a matched set. They were a little bit plastic, a little too chiseled, and were all smiling like they expected Keagan and Cassie to come running. Not to mention they looked like they had more product in their hair than Cassie did. *No thank you.*

"I kind of want to take my time," she said. She fin-gered the high hem of her dress, then let it go. Again.

"I think you might be stalling," Keagan teased her. "You haven't even kissed *one* boy yet!"

"The summer is young!" Cassie protested. "I'm just getting started!"

"Excuses, excuses," Keagan said, shaking her head as if scolding Cassie. "We made a pact, you know. I'm already up to four!"

"Four?" Cassie demanded. She led Keagan deeper into the club. The place opened up into a vast cavern of a dance floor—filled with glittering, gyrating people. The energy level was high and the beat was cranking. "When did you get four?" Cassie continued, shouting into Keagan's ear. "You just said there were only three!"

"This guy I hung out with one night after work," Keagan said with a shrug and a coy little smile. "He's kind of a friend of a friend, I guess. I forgot."

"You are bad," Cassie told her.

"And you're definitely stalling," Keagan threw right back at her. "This is a prime opportunity to kiss more guys. I know I plan to!"

Cassie just laughed. She couldn't hold back any longer, so she and Keagan hit the dance floor. It felt amazing to let go, to lose herself in the music.

After a few songs, Keagan pantomimed her need for a drink, so Cassie let her lead the way off the floor, though she was reluctant to go.

"It's way too hot in here!" Keagan cried in Cassie's ear. Instead of approaching the bar at the back, Keagan maneuvered through the crowd and led Cassie out into the club's vast, multitiered back patio. People stood in clusters, some smoking, some lounging across benches scattered at regular intervals. There were two additional bars on the patio—but the best part was how deliciously cool the night air felt against Cassie's skin after all that dancing.

They got two bottles of water and snagged a bench, and were sighing with happiness when two cute guys walked up.

"You two look like you're having fun," the first one said. He had a warm, open smile and freckles that somehow worked with his curly blond hair. Cassie couldn't help but admire someone who used his freckles to his advantage, having despaired over her own for so long.

"It's summer," Cassie said. She and Keagan grinned at each other. "Of course we're having fun."

The second guy had darker hair, and was both better looking in a classical way and preppier than his friend. He stepped up, eyeing Keagan with stark appreciation.

"I hear that," he said. "I live for summer. Freshman year at Occidental kicked our asses."

"Speak for yourself," the first guy said with a laugh. He rolled his eyes at Cassie. "My buddy Ty here found it hard to get out of bed before four in the afternoon. But some of us had early labs, so we adjusted." His smile widened when Cassie laughed appreciatively. "I'm Colin," he said.

"I'm Penelope," Keagan said from beside Cassie. Cassie whipped her head around to look at her, and caught her friend smirking slightly.

"It's nice to meet you, Penelope," Ty said, moving even closer to Keagan.

It hadn't occurred to Cassie to make up a totally new identity, but she liked the idea. She could create a girl to match the dress she was wearing. A Greta-esque version of Cassie, who would dance her ass off and strut with confidence and start taking her Project Kiss responsibilities seriously. She smiled. The way her alter ego would.

"I'm Delilah," she told the two guys, remembering from honors English that Delilah was supposed to be a temptress of biblical proportions. Like, literally. And besides, she'd loved that Plain White T's song so much she'd practically considered having the lyrics tattooed on her body.

"That's a beautiful name," Colin said, and Cassie agreed with him. She wanted to be the Delilah that she imagined with perfect clarity: wicked, powerful, sexy, and carefree.

"Want to dance?" Cassie asked Colin, shooting a sideways glance at "Penelope." She no longer cared if her dress was too short. She wanted it to be too short. She noticed Colin looking at her legs, and made sure her hips swung when she moved. Because that was how Delilah rolled.

"I would love to dance," Colin said—which made Ty snort with laughter. She saw Ty give his friend a look that clearly said, *Since when do you dance?* Cassie figured everybody was playing some kind of game tonight. Why not run with it and see what the night held in store?

"Then let's dance," she said, and she took Colin's hand as she led him toward the dance floor.

✦ ✦ ✦

By the time the club's lights came on, they were exhausted. And Cassie had found out a lot about Colin. He and Ty were frat brothers and roommates. Colin was originally from Florida, but he didn't see moving back there after college—he liked California. He was the oldest of three kids, wished he could have brought his dog with him to school, wanted to be a doctor someday, and knew he was a terrible dancer but was willing to keep trying anyway.

In return, Cassie had told him nothing about herself. When he'd asked a question, she'd tossed her hair and refused to answer, with a sexy smirk. She'd had a blast. She loved being Delilah, who was flirtatious and daring and was happy to rub up against him one minute and then laughingly shimmy away the next. There was no getting close. No telling stories. She let him buy her a few drinks and didn't even try to pay for them herself.

She laughed and danced and was actually disappointed when the night came to an end.

Colin walked her toward the valet. Up ahead, Ty and "Penelope" were leaning into each other and making out as they walked.

Colin took one of Cassie's hands, and pulled her around to face him.

Cassie looked up at him—at his broad face with the sprinkling of freckles and the mischievous grin—and she knew that he was going to kiss her.

Finally.

He leaned down, fitting his mouth to hers. Cassie felt excitement speed through her body, and the kiss deepened. Cassie closed her eyes and swayed closer, not caring that they were in a crowded parking lot. Not even caring when his hands smoothed along her back, tracing the line of her spine. He was hot, and this had been coming all night. Cassie felt electric. On fire.

The kiss kept going. Colin put his hand on the back of Cassie's head. His hand was hot and sweaty and as his mouth moved across hers, Cassie found herself wondering how much kissing was required to count toward her summer total. Did she actually have to fully make out with these guys? Or was a single kiss acceptable? She and the girls were going to have to hammer out some details.

Colin was still kissing her, and Cassie began to notice how he was breathing kind of funny through his nose.

And how he moved his tongue in her mouth. She noticed it in a clinical, detached way, which made everything feel awkward.

Why am I still kissing him?

It was an excellent question. Cassie pulled away and smiled a little guiltily at Colin when his unfocused eyes finally trained on her.

"Oh, um, thanks," she said. "I had a really good night."

"I'll call you," he said, and Cassie didn't bother to tell him that she hadn't given him her number.

She waited until he turned around, and then she let out the laughter that had been fighting to escape. She wiped her mouth, wrinkling her nose a little bit.

Oh well. They weren't supposed to be looking for soul mates.

One down, nine to go!

Chapter Eight

◆

"I don't know why today is so slow," Billy said, leaning over the counter at the bike shop. He sounded as annoyed as Cassie had been feeling all morning. "I consulted the runes last night and I thought they were telling me this would be a momentous day. Maybe my chakras are blocked. How do your chakras feel?"

Cassie looked up from her seat in the "business center"—what Billy called the desk and computer he'd tucked into a space barely big enough to be a supply closet. She'd spent the morning trolling the Internet to pass the time, catching up on old television recaps and reading articles on Jezebel, not to mention Twittering incessantly about how slow work was. It was hard to sit around when she was used to spending her mornings biking. It was actually painful.

"My chakras are fine," she said, rolling her eyes at Billy. She sighed. "It doesn't make any sense that we're not busy. It's a beautiful day! *Everyone* can't want to shop, can they?"

Billy's eyes crinkled up in the corners when he smiled, as if his skin wanted to be out in the sun even when he was indoors.

"Tourists," he joked. "Always pains in the ass."

Cassie laughed appreciatively. Getting to know Billy as more than just her mother's old friend had been one of the extra perks of her job so far. She'd always thought that he was kind of weird, what with the long ponytail and the layers of necklaces, to say nothing of the tie-dye and the Grateful Dead obsession, so she hadn't expected him to be *funny.*

"Why don't you head off to lunch early?" Billy said now. "No point in you sitting around here if you don't have to. Go flirt with the divers down at Casino Point."

"Ew," Cassie said, laughing. "Do I look like I need dating advice?"

"I've been dating for almost thirty-five years," Billy retorted. "What I don't know about dating isn't worth knowing." He grinned, and Cassie wondered—not for the first time—if there was more going on with the equally crunchy baker lady across the street than he let on.

"And last I checked, you were still single," Cassie pointed out, standing up. "So the dating isn't working out too well, is it?" She decided not to mention that she'd noticed how happy Billy got whenever Roberta dropped by with special deliveries of scones.

"Depends on whether you think the purpose of dating is to find someone and settle down, or simply to date," Billy said with a wink. Then he shooed her out of the shop. She heard him crank up the stereo behind her. It sounded like Pink Floyd, which always meant Billy was feeling blue.

Cassie thought about Billy's questionable wisdom as she walked down the street toward Crescent, which she could see was bustling with tourists—none of whom wanted a bike tour, apparently. She laughed a little bit when she realized how warped she was. Her friends would rejoice if they somehow didn't have to work for half a day, and here she was moping about it. She was certifiable. This was summer! She was supposed to want to slack off and laze around.

Cassie laughed at herself again. That wasn't her at all. She liked to *do* things. She'd never understood how people could just lie on a beach all day. She got bored after half a magazine or three songs on her iPod, whichever came first. She would much rather go on a long hike. Just as much sun, without the tedium of lying still for hours, doing absolutely nothing.

She reached Crescent and stood still for a minute, taking in the breeze off the bay and the clank of the riggings on the boats on their moorings. Did she want to walk up toward Casino Point, as Billy had suggested, and ogle the scuba divers at the underwater dive park? Or did she want to relax at her favorite café?

She decided to split the difference and do both—after all, she didn't have to be back at work for almost two hours. So she headed toward the dive park, half for the hot guys in tight-fitting scuba gear, and half because it was a nice walk and she still felt jittery from all the sitting still she'd done so far that day.

She had walked a little ways down the street when she stopped to look out over the harbor at the cruise ship sliding into view. It looked like it could scoop up the whole of the town of Avalon and carry it away, or maybe the whole island of Catalina. It was like a floating city. It was somewhere between monstrous and amazing.

Assuming it wasn't there to devour the island, Cassie hoped it was filled with people who thought an afternoon bike ride was the perfect way to spend their vacation.

Excited about the prospect of riders, Cassie decided to skip Casino Point—and any potential hot diver dates—in favor of a hearty lunch, so she could hurry back to the shop ahead of any possible customers.

She turned back around and saw Trey standing there,

maybe five feet away from her. Obviously following her.

He smiled—that devastating crook of his mouth, down in the corner of his lips.

Cassie felt her stomach do a backflip, as though his smile were connected directly to her body. She told herself that she wasn't thinking about kissing *him* specifically. It was a side effect of Project Kiss—she was always thinking about kissing. That sexy smile had nothing to do with it.

But he was still standing there. Watching her. He silently mouthed, "Hey," in her direction and raised an eyebrow. If she didn't stop staring soon, she was pretty sure her entire body would start to show the blush she could feel rising to her face. She didn't know what to do.

So she decided not to do anything. She frowned in his general direction and then walked off toward her favorite lunch place like she didn't notice he was there. At first she felt small, mean, and even rude. But then she remembered what Greta had said. She remembered his reputation. And that made her feel better about ignoring him. Like she was somehow ignoring him not just for her own sake, but for that of all the girls whom he'd played in the past.

She felt her stride pick up, like the power of not being made a fool of was rocking through her.

Cassie's timing was perfect. She walked into her favorite café, nestled into the corner of a building that looked out over the harbor, just as the cruise ship docked. That meant she would get in ahead of the crowd that would soon be fighting for the best lunch spots all up and down Crescent. She chose a table with a view and smiled gratefully at the cute blond waiter when he presented her with her preferred iced tea without her having to order it.

"You're in here a lot," he said. "I like to take care of my regulars." He leaned against the table, grinning down at her. He was tall, and he filled out his white T-shirt almost too perfectly. His blond hair was a mess of curls, and his eyes were almost as blue as the Catalina sky.

"I work over at Billy's Bikes," she told him. "You'll probably see me just about every day—I love the food here." She sighed happily. "The Caesar wrap is like a gift from the gods!"

"I'll tell my boss," the waiter said, and then leaned in closer, pitching his voice low. "He's a complete diva about the food, so it'll score me some points. Always a good idea, since I can never manage to get here on time." He laughed. "I like my sleep."

"I'm Cassie," she told him, because she needed a Catalina friend—especially if Trey Carter was now following her around. "And I'm happy to help you score points."

"Ryan," he said, smiling so she could see his adorable dimples, one in each cheek.

"Nice to meet you," she said. "You're my first Catalina summer friend! So far, I've basically only hung out with Billy from the shop, who's nice but like fifty years old, and the people who take my bike tour."

"Unacceptable," Ryan said with a laugh. "You need to come hang out at the coffeehouse up on the hill sometime." He waved in the general direction of the hills and named an address. "Farther from Crescent and therefore fewer tourists. Nothing but summer friends!"

"Billy thinks I need to hang out down at Casino Point," Cassie said. "Why am I not surprised that his advice is out-of-date?"

"Oh, to flirt with the cute diver boys?" Ryan asked. He grinned. "A tried and true Catalina pastime. One I indulge in myself every now and again. You definitely can't hide any flaws in a wet suit. It's almost as much fun as going to West Hollywood on a Saturday night."

Well, that explained the utter lack of flirtatiousness in their conversation. Which had been practically unheard of in the ten-boy summer so far! Cassie probably should have guessed why even before he mentioned West Hollywood, L.A.'s trendy gay neighborhood.

"I must be missing out if *everyone* thinks the dive park is the go-to hot boy destination," she said. "I almost went there today, but opted for eating instead. Obviously a big mistake."

"Wet suits," Ryan said,
He raised his eyebrows at
bodies. End of discussio

He walked over to an
laughing to herself.

The café filled up quickly. The c
the giant cruise ship made a beeline fo
restaurants along Crescent Avenue. Cassie saw
in, and made a huge show of studying her menu
he walked by, as if she hadn't even noticed him.

But she could feel him—his nearness. It was like an infuriating prickle on the back of her neck. Why was he on Catalina again? What did he want? Why was he following her around when she was trying to ignore him? Cassie was torn between the part of her that wanted to see his behavior as romantic—and the part of her that grimly repeated Greta's words over and over, trying to make them sink in. Greta wouldn't lie. Trey was exactly what she said he was, and the fact that he had kissable-looking lips just made his games more regrettable.

If only Cassie didn't have to practically chant it to herself to get it through her apparently thick head.

The most embarrassing part was that she *wanted* to turn around and let her eyes drink him in. She wanted to talk to him again and see if she would feel that same spellbinding ease all over again. Or, at the very least, she wanted to go over and prove, once and for all, that the

seemed so perfect had just been about
the first party of the summer and the fact
had already been so happy. It hadn't been
m at all. It didn't mean there was any particular
stry between them.

Ryan came back to her table, and Cassie was grateful
or the distraction.

"I'm going to change it up and order the South-
western Salad," she told Ryan. "And please don't feel
you have to skimp on the buttermilk dressing."

"That's the best part!" Ryan agreed. He scribbled on
his pad and then leaned close to Cassie again. "And
speaking of cute boys . . ."

"Yes?" she asked, laughing. "Aren't we always speaking of cute boys?"

"We should be," Ryan murmured.

"Then please," Cassie said, gesturing grandly. "Go
ahead."

"The one at the table behind you is staring at you,"
Ryan said. "Has been since he walked in, all smoldering
and dark-eyed. Very Chuck Bass, but with a much more
summer-friendly wardrobe. I approve." He paused. "And
he paid for your lunch."

Cassie stared up at Ryan's blue eyes, her stomach
twisting. She was touched for about thirty seconds. But
why would Trey buy her lunch? What game was he playing? *Oh, right,* she reminded herself. *This* is *his game.*

She knew that Trey was staring—she could feel it. But she knew he couldn't see her face. So she rolled her eyes so only Ryan could see. Then, she reached out and put a hand on Ryan's well-sculpted arm and let it roam a little bit upwards in a caress. She also tossed her head the way she'd seen Greta do—in fact, she'd studied the way Greta did it. Toss the head, then gaze adoringly. Cassie did both—and then let her fingers roam even farther, testing out the shape of Ryan's bicep. Which was, as it happened, maybe the most perfect bicep she'd ever touched.

Ryan blinked down at her for a moment.

"You're silly," Cassie said, in her flirtiest possible voice. "You're the only one I ever look at."

"Of course I am," Ryan said smoothly, flashing his dimples. He collected Cassie's menu in one swoop, then leaned over to take her face in one hand. He pulled her close, then kissed her sweetly—lingeringly—on the forehead.

It should have looked like everything it wasn't. Cassie was pretty confident that it had, especially when Ryan glanced at the table behind her and laughed.

Take that, Trey, Cassie thought in triumph.

She didn't look around once for the rest of her lunch hour. And she enjoyed every last bite of the food he'd bought her.

Chapter Nine

◆

The party was insane. It was a Friday night in mid-July, and it seemed as if all of Hollywood had turned up, dressed to kill.

Cassie thought it was like something out of *The Hills*. Completely scene-obsessed girls in as little clothing as possible, surrounded by super-trendy boys, all packed into one of this month's hottest clubs on Sunset.

"How do you know these people?" Cassie asked Keagan, who was sucking on her bright yellow drink through a straw and swaying slightly to the music.

"Not me," Keagan said. She shrugged. "Greta."

Greta, however, could not be questioned, as she'd peeled off immediately after they'd arrived, claiming she needed to do some reconnaissance work.

"I would not be surprised to see Heidi and Spencer walk in the door," Cassie said with a giggle. "And to be honest, K, I don't know if I'd think that was really cool or horribly lame."

Keagan laughed. "I hear you," she said. Then she made a face. "I wish Heidi would walk in here. I have a lot of questions for her. Okay, just one. Why is she still with that loser?"

"Such a controlling jerk," Cassie agreed.

They were discussing the intricacies of the Heidi and Spencer relationship when Greta strolled back up, a drink in her hand and a noticeably bored look on her face. Of course, the over-it expression only made her look hotter.

"What are we talking about?" she asked.

"*The Hills*," Keagan said.

"Heidi and Spencer," Cassie said. "Specifically, how Spencer is evil."

"Totally," Greta said dismissively. "But I think he's, like, encouraged to act that way. I think they make him. It makes the show better."

"Are you defending Spencer Pratt?" Cassie asked, laughing. "The most revolting guy alive?"

"I'm just saying that there's more to it, that's all," Greta said. She reached over and slapped the remains of her drink down on the bar. "Are you guys ready to go? This party is a snore."

"Really?" Keagan looked surprised. "We've been here maybe twelve minutes."

"Plus there are tons of boys," Cassie pointed out. "And we have a quota to reach."

"That's the thing," Greta said. She sighed. "I've kissed all of these boys already."

Cassie and Keagan looked at each other, then gaped at Greta.

"All of them?" Keagan echoed. "*All* of them?"

"Like—*every single one*?" Cassie asked, in the same astounded tone. "There have to be a hundred people here, Greta. At least fifty of them are guys. You kissed *all* of them?" Surely that was impossible. Surely that much kissing would lead to chapped lips, at the very least. Or would somehow affect Greta a bit more than her nonchalant position against the bar would suggest. She lounged there with one Acne jeans–clad hip jutting out, which drew attention to her long legs and her badass heels. She looked exactly like the vamp she claimed to be. Cassie didn't know whether to applaud—or be a little bit afraid of her.

Greta shrugged. "Well, all the kissable ones, yeah," she said. She made a face as she cast a look around.

"Sure," Cassie said, after sharing another look with Keagan, who only widened her eyes in astonishment. "We can go. Where to?"

"There has to be another party somewhere," Greta

said. "It's a Friday night in July in L.A. There should be at least a million parties to choose from."

"There's that thing down in Long Beach," Keagan offered. "Though it's a little bit of a drive, it could be cool."

"Ugh, no," Greta said with a shudder. "Not the heavy metal thing."

"Some guys I know are in a band," Keagan explained to Cassie. "*Not* a heavy metal band. They're playing at this place that we've been to before—"

"This sticky, skanky club, ew," Greta interjected, shaking her head. "And the whole groupie scene is so not us, K. Boys should be throwing their shirts at us, not the other way around."

"We went to one show three years ago," Keagan said, again to Cassie. "Greta still hasn't recovered."

"That horrible girl threw a beer at me!" Greta cried. "I had *beer* all over me, Cassie!"

"She walked into the mosh pit," Keagan retorted—to Cassie, though the edge in her voice was all for Greta. "I don't think she can claim it was a deliberate attack!"

"Deliberate or not, I still had to stand in the shower for three days to get the stink off me," Greta snapped at her.

Cassie had to do something before her friends got into a brawl right there at the bar—over something that had happened ages ago!

"I know of a party," she said, which immediately silenced both of them.

"Do tell," Greta practically purred.

"I really wasn't planning to go," Cassie said. "This friend of my ex is throwing it, and to be honest, I was surprised I even got invited. I think he might have clicked on my name by mistake when he was making the Facebook invite, you know?"

"Cassie, please," Greta said, reaching over and slinging an arm around Cassie's neck. "Three hot girls at your party is never a mistake, no matter if it's expected or not. Let's go!"

✦ ✦ ✦

A half hour later, as they approached what they hoped was the address in Laurel Canyon for the third time—having gotten lost along the twisting mountain roads twice already before finding the familiar Laurel Canyon Country Store and starting over—Cassie was feeling nervous. She wished she could tell Greta and Keagan that she'd changed her mind. But they were both so excited, the near-squabble in the club forgotten between them as they giggled over their summer adventures so far. How could she ask them to forgo a party just because she was suddenly freaking out?

"Why did you pick the name Penelope?" Greta was

asking, laughing so hard as she navigated her sporty BMW convertible down the narrow road that Cassie, in the backseat and staring at the uncomfortably close drop-off into the steep canyon, closed her eyes and said a quick prayer that the car didn't go over the side.

"I don't know," Keagan said, her laugh turning into a little snort. "It was so random! But he couldn't remember my name at the end of the night anyway, so it was a wasted effort!"

"Did you give him a phone number?" Greta wiped at her eyes. "Because I have to screen all my calls. Like, religiously, at this point."

"Like you ever don't screen your calls in the first place," Keagan scoffed.

Cassie tuned them out. What was she so worried about? Yes, the party was being thrown by Daniel Fletcher's friend, Gage Pearson. She was astonished to realize she hadn't thought about Daniel in some time. Not completely forgotten about him, of course. She just hadn't remembered to be upset about him and the things he could be up to with who-knew-which-girl in Europe. Was that progress?

Cassie let the canyon night air sweep over her. Jasmine and eucalyptus, with an underlying kick of rosemary. The air was just cool enough to be noticeable, but warm enough that Cassie didn't mind that all she was wearing was the thinnest of T-shirts over a tiny little skirt. It was another splendid night in her city, and she was up in the glorious Hollywood Hills, where every curve in the road opened up over the endless stretch of lights reaching out to the horizon that, altogether, made up Los Angeles. It was beautiful.

She told herself she didn't care that she was going to a party at Gage Pearson's parents' house. Gage Pearson, who was a great friend of Daniel's and who Cassie worried would mock her for the way Daniel had dropped her so carelessly. Or worse, pity her. Either way, she came out looking pathetic, and that was completely unfair, because Daniel was seriously old news to her now. But would anyone from Siskiyou Academy—especially buddies of Daniel's—believe that?

At least her friends would be with her, she thought, trying to relax as Greta parked along the side of the road. She didn't have to do this alone.

Cassie led the way inside the boxy modern house, trying to rustle up a bravado that she didn't necessarily feel. After all, if Gage or anyone else from Siskiyou was inclined to pity or mock, she couldn't let them think she'd been moping around since school ended. Especially since she hadn't been doing anything of the kind.

The house was already packed with people, most of them congregating around the television in the big family room playing Rock Band, or hanging out by the keg out back. There was a den with a Ping-Pong table—and a tournament under way. In the vast kitchen, there were sofas surrounding a fireplace at one end and the usual appliances at the other. In the middle of the room, a group of girls Cassie vaguely recognized from school—freshmen maybe—danced in a circle to Katy Perry. Cassie smiled at the handful of people she knew from Siskiyou Academy, made a little small talk with Gage Pearson himself, and was profoundly relieved when everyone seemed as disinclined to discuss Daniel as she was.

Thank goodness.

"Is that a smile?" Keagan teased her when Cassie flopped down next to her on one of the overstuffed suede couches near the fireplace. "You've been tense since we got here."

"Where's Greta?" Cassie asked. Keagan waved her hand toward the back of the house.

"Some guy named Phil claimed he had a cool tattoo in an interesting place," she said. "That was pretty much that." She gazed at Cassie. "Are you avoiding the question?"

"No," Cassie said. "I didn't want to make a big deal out of it, but I was kind of worried that people would think I was pathetic because of the whole Daniel thing."

Keagan frowned. "What? Why? *He's* the loser!"

Cassie grinned at the support. "You know how it is,"

she said. She checked over her shoulder to make sure no one from school was near enough to hear her. "Daniel's like a god to some of these people. And this is his friend's house, so—"

"Did someone say something?" Keagan demanded, sitting up and scowling ferociously. Cassie knew without a doubt that if she said yes, Keagan would run over and defend Cassie's honor, no questions asked.

"No one seems to care," Cassie said, with a big sigh of relief. "Happily. As we walked in, it occurred to me that Gage might have invited me deliberately, you know? Just to mess with me."

"That would be crazy," Keagan said, relaxing back against the couch. She snickered. "You watch way too much *Gossip Girl*."

"Well, nobody turned into Blair Waldorf," Cassie said, and tapped Keagan's drink with her own in a spontaneous toast. "Which I think gives us reason to celebrate!"

"Count me in!" Keagan cried.

They decided to celebrate by dominating the Ping-Pong table tournament. They'd been playing together since they were small, so they worked up a natural doubles rhythm, and destroyed the competition. First it was a couple, a super-intense emo guy and his frail, pierced girlfriend. Cassie smashed a serve down the center of the table and had to choke back a laugh when the girlfriend missed it completely, almost whacking her boyfriend instead.

"Concentrate, Chelsea," he hissed at her.

"Ping-Pong is a rough sport," Cassie murmured in an aside to Keagan. "You have to focus."

They had to stop looking at each other. Every time they met eyes, they started cracking up.

"We rule!" Keagan crowed after a particularly tough game against two sporty-looking girls from the Valley.

"You're like some diabolical Ping-Pong version of the Williams sisters," one of the defeated girls groaned.

"We totally rule," Cassie agreed. "And all this ruling is making me thirsty."

"I'll wait here," Keagan said, and Cassie laughed when she saw that her friend's attention was fixed on one of the guys who'd been watching them play Ping-Pong. She saw the way he ran his eyes up and down Keagan's body, and left them to it.

She was refilling her drink from the keg out back when she noticed that one of the guys standing nearby was checking her out. Cassie loved how good that made her feel. Just by being herself, and by not being afraid to go to a party where Daniel's friends *might* have made her feel like a loser. She would have refused to do that a few months ago. She was different now.

And the different version of Cassie had no trouble checking the guy out in return. He wore a button-down shirt and scruffy khaki shorts. Half surfer and half preppy, with close-cut dirty-blond hair and a swagger that she couldn't help but smile at as he crossed to her side.

"I'm Brad," he said. "And I can't believe we haven't been introduced."

"Well, Brad," Cassie said with a smile, feeling like so much confidence deserved a little teasing in return, "what makes you think I'm looking to make new acquaintances? Maybe I have too many friends already."

Behind him, she saw Gage Pearson and a bunch of other guys from Siskiyou watching the interaction, and it gave her another boost. There was nothing even remotely pathetic about her tonight.

"None of them are me," Brad replied, his grin widening.

Cassie leaned a little closer, and loved it when he did the same, closing the distance between them so she could smell the soap he'd used in the shower. Brad wasn't tall; he was about Cassie's height and built like a wrestler—low and compact.

And Cassie knew without a doubt that he'd be the next kiss on her list.

"Okay, then," she said. She wondered what kind of kisser he'd be—how his mouth would feel against hers. She saw that knowing look in his eyes. "Then I guess you'd better tell me all about you."

"Everything was boring," Brad said, his grin widening. "Until tonight. Tonight is when things started to get interesting."

Talk about lame lines. He was lucky she had a weakness for that beachy-preppy look. Cassie decided to punish him.

"What makes you think I want to waste my time with someone who admits he's totally boring when I'm not around?" she teased him, angling her body a little bit closer to his. "I already know that *I'm* interesting."

"Ouch," he said. He laughed. "I can see I need to bring my A game with you."

"You mean that wasn't A game?" Cassie replied, grinning. "Now I'm insulted." Thinking about games made her think about Trey Carter—but she brushed away thoughts of Christopher Pike books and Trey's unselfconscious joy on his bike, and concentrated on Brad instead.

He clutched at his heart and staggered back a step or two. "You're killing me," he told her. "And you still haven't told me your name."

Cassie smiled at him. She stepped over and took his arm, admiring his tight, smooth skin.

"I'm Cassie," she said, tilting her head as she looked at him. "And you look like you can take it."

Chapter Ten

✦

"Tell me why we're doing this again?" Keagan asked, her forehead all scrunched up as she leaned forward from the backseat of Greta's convertible. "Because I don't know about you guys, but I'm, uh, not going to be applying to UCLA this fall. I'd never get in, not in a million years."

"So not the point," Greta singsonged from the driver's seat, turning left off of Sunset Boulevard across from the Bel Air archway, and shooting into the UCLA campus.

"The point is boys, K," Cassie said, turning around in her seat to face Keagan. She grinned. "College boys today, to change it up."

"But . . . it's summer," Keagan protested. "Why

would there be any college boys around in the summer?"

"Keagan, get a grip," Greta said, laughing. "This is UCLA, not some puny arts college nestled away in the woods somewhere. There's always something going on here!"

"Lots of training for athletics starts in the summer," Cassie told Keagan, with only a little less over-the-top boisterousness than Greta had just displayed. "Among other things."

"Why do you know so much about UCLA?" Keagan asked Cassie, her eyes widening. "Are you going to apply here? *Can* you apply here without being, like, laughed out of the admissions office?"

"K, seriously—this is not the time for stressing about college applications," Greta said as she parked the car. She swiveled around to eye Keagan. "You need to think about fun, not the future, okay?"

Cassie climbed out of the passenger seat, glad that she hadn't had to answer Keagan's questions about UCLA. The truth was, Cassie wasn't entirely sure where she wanted to apply to college, but UCLA was on the list. She just wasn't sure if she should stay in her hometown. Maybe she should head to the East Coast, to one of those famous, storied places she'd been hearing about her whole life. Sometimes she fantasized about stately brick buildings covered with ivy, or East Coast seasons. But that was only a daydream. Cassie wasn't sure she could handle being so far away from home. As the three girls stepped out of the dark parking garage into the bright sunlight, Cassie thrust the thoughts away. Greta was right. There would be time to worry about the future in the fall. This was summer. This was about *now*.

It had been Greta's idea to take Project Kiss out for a romp in the bright light of day. Cassie and Keagan teased her that this had more to do with her regret that Interesting Tattoo Guy at Gage Pearson's party hadn't been nearly as good a kisser as she'd expected than with any desire to go collegiate. Whatever the reason, Greta had decreed that everyone's day off was a perfect time to explore the delights of college guys.

And where better to do that than UCLA, L.A.'s prettiest campus?

The soaring brick buildings, the steep steps, the green lawns, and the big Bruin statue Cassie had climbed on as a kid. As long as she could remember, she'd spent a weekend every April wandering around the *Los Angeles Times* Festival of Books that took over the campus. She loved being back on campus now. She could practically inhale the energy of the place.

She checked out her friends, who had each interpreted "college visit" in a different way. Greta had pulled out black-rimmed glasses, a beret, and a flirty little plaid schoolgirl skirt. She was even sporting a pair of pulled-up kneesocks. The result was half anime character, half Catholic schoolgirl, and a hundred percent adorable. Keagan, meanwhile, had clearly freaked.

"Is that your 'I'm responsible, I swear!' outfit?" Cassie asked her, trying not to laugh, out of loyalty.

Keagan sighed, but her cheeks reddened. "I didn't know what to wear!" she wailed.

"You look good," Greta said soothingly. "Very pulled together."

Keagan looked very Blair Waldorf—a preppy, fussy sort of look that was totally at odds with her laid-back surfer chick vibe. She was sporting a navy headband over a matching white shift dress with navy trim, with navy and gold flats. She looked manicured and pressed—and very unlike Keagan.

Cassie hadn't really gone for a whole new look. They were just here to walk around campus—she didn't have to worry about impressing anyone. So she'd stuck with jeans and a T-shirt. Granted, it was her nicest pair of jet-black J Brand jeans and a super-cute royal blue top she'd found at Zara, so she wasn't exactly bumming. But she had maintained her own look, unlike her friends, which gave her a little confidence boost.

"I have a surprise," Greta announced as they climbed to the top of Janss Steps, all eighty-seven of them, panting a little bit. Cassie looked over her shoulder at the great expanse of the steps that led down to the Fowler Museum, at the trees and the rolling green grass all the way down the hill. Students were lying in the sun, or kicking soccer balls around. A couple of guys in Bruins T-shirts were eating under the shade of one of the trees. Cassie let herself imagine that she was a part of it for a moment.

Then she focused on Keagan's dubious expression.

"What kind of surprise?" she asked Greta.

"We aren't just here to wander around and meet people," Greta announced grandly. "We're taking a prospective student tour."

Keagan looked stricken. "Greta! I told you, I can't take a tour here!"

"Why is a college campus any different from a guy?" Greta asked airily as she set off across Dickson Plaza. Cassie and Keagan had no choice but to follow in her wake. "You have to test them out to see if they fit," Greta continued with a little twirl, complete with a saucy look over her shoulder.

"I already know I don't fit," Keagan muttered, crossing her arms over her chest and rounding her shoulders as if to make herself shrink from view. Cassie nudged her with her hip.

"Look how pretty this place is," she said, nodding toward Royce Hall on one side and Powell Library on the other. "Just relax and enjoy."

✦ ✦ ✦

Cassie had to remind herself of her own advice when she and Keagan were standing at the back of the group of prospective students a little bit later, shuffling along on the campus tour. Everyone else seemed so serious. One girl was jotting down notes as the tour guide spoke. Another guy was muttering into a voice recorder. Cassie felt kind of guilty that she was taking the tour as an attempt to meet cute boys. Was that the most shallow thing ever? What did that say about her?

Greta did not seem similarly troubled. She'd left Cassie and Keagan in her dust, and was flitting from one attractive prospective student to the next, fluttering her lashes and talking in what Cassie was pretty sure was a French accent.

"I am from ze *Pear-eeee*," Greta purred at the cutest guy in the pack—a long, lanky boy who'd announced at the start of the tour he was from Maryland. "But I like ze California."

"*Ze California,*" Cassie repeated, trying to hide her giggle behind her hand.

"She's nuts," Keagan muttered, still looking as if she were attending her own execution. "Why do I go along with everything she says? Like some *sheep* or something?"

"*Excusez-moi!*" Greta cried then, interrupting the tour

guide and casting a significant look at her friends. "Did you say something about ze football team? Where do they practice? Exactly?"

"Bruins practice hasn't started yet," the tour guide said, frowning at Greta. "It's usually the first week in August." Cassie knew that if the unamused tour guide had said, "Oh, they're practicing right now," Greta would have bailed on the tour without a second thought.

"Merde," Greta muttered. She smiled winningly when Maryland Guy turned to look at her. She coughed. *"Merci,"* she said in a louder voice.

"You're not a sheep," Cassie said reassuringly to Keagan, stifling a giggle. She wasn't sure why Keagan was freaking out, but she knew it wasn't Greta's fault. "And we do what she says because she's fun. Left to our own devices, we'd be sitting in our bedrooms all summer lighting candles to the memories of our exes."

"Gah." Keagan made a face to go with the gagging noise. "That's a horrible image."

"It's true and you know it." Cassie nodded in Greta's direction. Their friend was twirling that skirt of hers around, practically pirouetting in front of Maryland Guy, who looked dazed and smitten. "I mean, look at her! She makes everything more fun."

"I know," Keagan said with a sigh. She finally uncrossed her arms from her chest and looked at Cassie.

"Every time I think about colleges and the fact I have to choose one and then, you know, *go there*–" She stopped and waved a hand in the air. "I mean, look at everyone. They're so much more–I don't know–*ready*."

Cassie frowned. "I think everyone on this tour is a junior in high school," she said. "And I think the girls up front are in eighth grade."

"Not just the tour." Keagan sighed, and then her words poured out. "All the students wandering around. Everyone looks really mature. I don't feel like that, and I don't see how I'm going to in, like, one year. What if I'm not college material?"

"Why wouldn't you be college material?" Cassie asked, shaking her head at her friend. "When did you become the dumb blond? Is that how you see yourself?"

"No," Keagan said, although her tone was unsure. "I don't know. College is a whole different thing. And I feel like I barely have high school under control, you know?"

"I do know," Cassie said reassuringly. Her efforts to bolster Keagan's self-esteem were put on pause when two guys who had been walking ahead of them slowed down and flanked the two girls. Cassie shot Keagan a quick look and then smiled brightly at the guy nearest her.

"Hello there, how y'all doin'?" she asked in her best Southern twang. "I'm Mae Rose Sugarbaker."

Cassie made sure not to look over at Keagan, though she could hear her friend attempting to cover a crack-up.

"I love Southern accents," the guy said, making serious eye contact with Cassie, his brown eyes twinkling. He smiled sweetly. "I'm Ricky."

"What are you all doin' in *Lost Ange-leez*?" Cassie asked, drawling like she was Scarlett O'Hara.

"Zis is a very different place than ze Paris, *oui*," she heard Greta saying in that French accent.

Cassie looked over at Keagan, who'd brightened, clearly restored by the attentions of the very good-looking auburn-haired guy who was hanging on her every word. Every one of which she was speaking in a crisp British accent.

"I do love London," Keagan said, in full British character, "but life can't always be scones and tea, can it?"

Cassie burst into laughter, which confused Ricky.

"Is something funny?" he asked, looking around.

"Not at all," Cassie drawled, trying her best to seem as Southern as chicken-fried steak. "I'm just happy to be here with y'all."

✦ ✦ ✦

When the prospectives were let loose in the campus store at the end of the tour, Greta beckoned the other two over to huddle near a display of Bruins memorabilia. Cassie wasn't sure why anyone would need a dining set emblazoned with the Bruins insignia, but it was nice to know the UCLA store sold them if she ever had such a need. She sidled in between her friends and pretended to gaze at the dessert plates.

"I had no idea you could do a Southern accent, Cassie!" Greta giggled. "I'm very impressed."

"Did I see you *nuzzling* that guy from Maryland?" Keagan demanded of Greta. "By the chemistry building?"

"It seemed appropriate," Greta said, patting her strawberry blond curls. Cassie laughed. "I wish I'd known when football practice was starting," Greta continued. "We're only missing it by a week! I guess we can come back."

"Um, no thanks," Keagan said. "The guy I was talking to wanted to compare SAT scores with me. Seriously."

"Tell him you got an 800 in French kissing," Greta replied. She smiled. "I don't think he'll care what you got on the verbal."

They all cracked up at that, but Cassie quickly shushed them, looking around for their tour guys—who might question why three girls from two different countries and the Deep South were whispering like the best of friends. The coast was clear.

"Where are we on Project Kiss numbers?" Greta asked. "Mr. Maryland is an excellent potential number five. Cassie?"

"I've kissed two so far," she said. Trey Carter's ridiculously sexy face appeared in her mind's eye for a second, but she blinked it away. Why did he always pop up at the most inconvenient times? "That guy at the club and then yummy Brad at Gage Pearson's party."

"It's almost August," Keagan chided her, giggling. "You need to get moving!"

"Says the girl who can't handle SAT Guy," Cassie retorted. "I'm moving along just fine, thank you."

"Just grab that guy and make it happen," Greta advised her. "You don't have to wait to be kissed, you know. Guys can be shy sometimes." She frowned at Keagan. "Are we even now? Score-wise?"

"I think I'm at six," Keagan said, trying to remember. "It could be five. I have to sit down and count everyone." She cocked her head toward the front of the store, where SAT Guy was buying a sweatshirt. "But not now."

Cassie and Greta watched as Keagan set off toward the cash registers, her shiny blond hair bouncing against her shoulders as she moved.

"Two?" Greta asked Cassie as Keagan moved in on her target. She turned and faced Cassie. "Only two since June? I'm ashamed for both of us."

Cassie desperately wanted to tell Greta about Trey's appearances on Catalina. But she knew Greta would be mad that she hadn't mentioned them when they had happened, and she knew that Greta would *definitely* be mad if Cassie claimed that Trey had anything to do with her low Project Kiss numbers. It sounded like Cassie was pining away for him.

And I'm not, she told herself fiercely.

"Let's call it three," she said, smirking at Greta. "I feel like I can tell the future today."

"Check you out," Greta said approvingly. "I'm so proud."

"You're about to be even prouder," Cassie boasted. She walked away from the Bruins china selection and scanned the store. She could see Ricky through the windows, standing in the sun-drenched courtyard, and quickly made her way outside.

"Mae Rose," he said when she stopped in front of him. "I thought you left."

"Now, would I leave without saying goodbye to the gentleman who accompanied me most of this tour?" Cassie asked, her drawl in full effect. "My mother would faint from shock. She raised me to be a good Southern girl, with manners." She stopped just short of saying, "I do declare." It would have been overkill.

"I haven't met a lot of Southern girls," Ricky said. His brown eyes looked like chocolate in the afternoon sunshine. "But I'm a big fan."

Cassie didn't say fiddle-dee-dee, either. Instead, she closed the distance between them and slid her hand around Ricky's neck. His skin was hot against her palm, and she could feel his soft curls against her fingers. His breath puffed against her cheeks, and she smiled. Then she stood on her toes and pressed her lips against his.

Ricky's mouth was warm and firm. He stood frozen for a moment; then his hands came to touch Cassie's waist and he leaned closer, his mouth pressing back against hers.

Cassie stood there for a moment and enjoyed it.

Then she stepped away and smiled up at him. She liked the way it felt to kiss him first. To move back first. To be in control. The kiss had been nice too.

"Wow," Ricky said. "I mean—thank you." Color darkened the skin above his cheekbones. "This has been the best college tour so far."

"Well, aren't you sweet," Cassie murmured, and then felt the Southern drawl take control. "I do declare."

She blamed it on the carefree feeling humming in her blood as she turned and walked away, grinning to herself.

Number three, and only seven left to go!

Chapter Eleven

✦

'm going to lunch!" Cassie called to Billy, locking her bike to its usual spot in the backyard space that served as their tour staging area and sometimes Billy's garage. The door to the repair part of the shop was open wide to catch the breeze coming up from the harbor below. Crosby, Stills, Nash & Young sang in perfect harmony from the stereo at only mildly deafening volume.

The older man didn't look up from the bike he was working on inside the repair center.

"Are you going to the café?" he asked.

"I can't seem to help myself," Cassie said with a pretend sigh. "It's too delicious."

Billy looked up then, and grinned. "Then you know you need to bring me one of those Caesar wraps," he said.

"Right?" Cassie threw out her hands. "They're addictive!"

"Maybe you should bring me two," Billy said, mulling it over. "I might need a snack later on."

Cassie hummed under her breath as she skipped down the road toward the café. She'd had a great morning. A tour that was tough at first—with an angry, gothed-out twelve-year-old girl—had ended up being terrific. Once Goth Lucy had relaxed a little bit and really taken in the view, Catalina had worked its magic on her. The whole family had left in a much better frame of mind than when they'd arrived. Cassie loved that she got to be a part of that. She knew that the ocean and the hills and the glorious sky did all the heavy lifting. But she liked to see that the beauty of the island got under everyone's skin, not just hers.

Cassie made her way down the bustling avenue toward the café, excited to tell Ryan all about her adventures at UCLA. She was trailing pretty far behind Keagan and Greta in Project Kiss, but Cassie wasn't worried. She felt like she'd just hit her stride. She'd been under the cloud that was her crush on Daniel Fletcher since the day she'd first arrived at Siskiyou Academy, but the way he'd dumped her had ended the crush as well as their relationship. It made her feel buoyant to be free of all that now. Cassie was working up to a full-on swagger when she ran up the steps into the café.

But she stopped dead in her tracks when she walked through the door and saw Trey standing there by the dessert case, chatting to Ryan.

As if they were the best of friends.

Cassie felt her mouth drop open in shock.

Ryan—the traitor—saw her come in and didn't leap away from Trey or run over to Cassie or do any of the other things Cassie thought would be appropriate responses to being caught speaking to the enemy. He kept talking to Trey as if it were perfectly normal. Cassie didn't know what to do. Should she ignore Trey when he was standing right there and talk to Ryan the way she usually did? Or should she just sit down and avoid the whole dilemma?

Cassie knew she was a coward. Greta would have marched over and given Trey a piece of her mind, kicked him out, and then slapped Ryan around too. She'd filled him in on all of the gory, terrible details about Trey's player past and almost-stalker present. How could he cavort with the enemy? But she couldn't bring herself to do anything except grab a table and pretend she wasn't at all bothered.

Ryan sauntered over a few minutes later—when, Cassie couldn't help but notice, Trey and he had finished talking and Trey had taken one of the high tables near the register. Ryan had in no way *hurried* over to Cassie.

"You are dead to me," Cassie told Ryan when he arrived. He laughed at her. He set down her drink and the salad she hadn't even completely decided she wanted yet. She glared at the food and told herself she wasn't sulking. She was rightly furious at Ryan's betrayal.

"You have to admire his tenacity, Cassie," Ryan said, as if he could read Cassie's mind. Then he smirked. "Especially when it comes in such a fine package."

Cassie rolled her eyes at him, and then noticed that he'd given her half a Caesar wrap too—clearly a peace offering.

"Are you trying to bribe away my legitimate outrage with this?" she asked, picking the wrap up and brandishing it at him. "Do you think it will work?"

"I am, and it will," Ryan said with all the lazy confidence in the world. He looked quickly over his shoulder and then dropped into the chair across from her. "You can't resist my charm. And I know you can't resist that Caesar wrap."

Cassie decided that Trey Carter and his suspicious appearances were not going to ruin her lunch—much less her friendship with Ryan. Also, Ryan was right. The delicious Caesar wrap cured all ills. So she let it go, and she and Ryan indulged in some serious dishing as she ate. It was one of the things she loved most about her job—these long, gossipy lunches with Ryan.

"What will you do if he calls you again?" she asked at

the conclusion of yet another scandalous tale, in which Ryan had gone on what he thought was a date only to discover the guy already had a boyfriend—the live-in, angry, and back-unexpectedly-from-his-trip kind.

"You know he will too," Ryan said with a sigh, as if being so good-looking and sought-after was a trial.

"They always call you again," Cassie agreed with a snicker.

"He can call all he wants," Ryan said, shaking his head. "Life is way too short for me to be jumping out of windows in West Hollywood. Seriously."

Cassie gathered her things together, including the two extra Caesar wraps for Billy, and leaned over to kiss Ryan on the cheek.

"I'll see you tomorrow," she said. And then she couldn't help herself—she looked over to Trey's table and was surprised to see that it was empty. Surprised and, if she was honest with herself, kind of let down. She ignored the feeling.

"Yes, you will," Ryan said cheerfully. "And one of these nights, you and I are going to have to have some adventures of our own!"

"You know it," Cassie called back. She could just imagine the trouble she and Ryan would get into on a night out. It would be fantastic.

Cassie headed out into the sunny afternoon, stopping in the doorway to slide her sunglasses over her eyes.

She was so busy fumbling with them as she started walking again that it took her a long moment or two to realize she was walking directly toward Trey. She blinked a few times in case she was imagining it, but no, he hadn't appeared in her mind again. He was right there.

He was leaning up against the side of the next building, watching her.

Waiting for her.

Cassie felt that strange confusion wash through her again. How could he look so good to her? How could her fingers actually twitch with the need to touch him—his glossy dark hair, maybe, or that half smile he always wore?

What was *wrong* with her?

"What are you doing?" Her voice sounded like someone else's, husky and weak. It sounded as confused as she felt, and she hated that he could hear it.

"What does it look like I'm doing?" he asked, pushing away from the wall and closing the distance between them. Cassie's heart began to pound inside her chest.

"I don't know," she said. She cleared her throat. "Following me around again?"

Trey smiled and held out his hand with his fingers closed over his palm, like he was holding something. Cassie stared at that hand as if she thought a poisonous tarantula might creep out of it. She looked up, and something in his dark eyes challenged her. Squaring her shoulders, she held out her hand, but flinched slightly when something dropped into it.

The hard plastic bubble was warm from contact with his skin. It was the kind of thing you could get from one of those machines at the arcade. A bright pink crown rattled around inside the plastic.

Your Majesty, he'd called her back at that party out in the Palisades. Cassie's throat tightened.

"Go out with me," he said.

She couldn't have heard that right. "What?"

"Go out with me," he repeated.

"I . . ." She stared at him, at his dark eyes that made her feel dizzy and his adorably crooked smile, and she wanted to. "I can't," she said. But her fingers closed over the crown in its plastic bubble, closing it in her fist.

"Of course you can," he said easily. He reached over as if he wanted to touch her, but he only dropped his hand again, leaving Cassie feeling strangely bereft. "Why not? What do you have to lose?"

In that moment, Cassie couldn't think of a single thing. Instead, she thought that maybe knowing how big a player he was would neutralize him. His usual games wouldn't work, right? She could play her own game. And no one had to know.

"Okay," she said. Though it sounded more like a whisper—or maybe that was just the roaring in her head. "Okay," she said again. "I'll do it."

Chapter Twelve

◆

Cassie couldn't believe she was actually doing this. She squinted at herself in the small mirror over the employee toilet in the back of bike shop and gave her hair another tousle on the off chance doing so would give it a little body.

Greta would be horrified. Cassie knew she would. And Cassie knew that she should be horrified herself—except that wasn't how she felt at all.

Because, she'd decided during her afternoon tour, she had this covered. She'd taken what Greta had told her to heart. She couldn't be played if she already knew the game. She was the one in control.

Cassie pulled the little red American Apparel dress out of her backpack and wondered if Keagan had been psychic when she'd suggested Cassie pack it "for emergencies."

"You never know when something might come up," she'd told Cassie. "And do you really want to go to some cool Catalina party in your bike shorts?"

Thank God for Keagan, she thought then, pulling the stretchy dress over her head. A *whole wardrobe in one dress,* Greta had called it when she'd encouraged Cassie to buy it. Cassie fussed around for a moment, finally deciding to wear it as a halter. The dark red material cupped her chest and swirled above her knees, making her feel flirty and delicious. A pair of flip-flops finished the outfit, and Cassie was amazed at how much prettier she felt just by changing her clothes. She looked at her reflection. When she was on her bike, unafraid to get grimy and really push herself, she felt tough and strong. And now, because she was wearing a pretty dress and about to meet a cute—if dangerous—boy for dinner, she felt a whole different kind of powerful.

Either way, she liked it.

Cassie let herself out the back of the bike shop, glad Billy had trusted her enough to give her a key. Okay, he'd trusted her within fifteen seconds, claiming he could read her *aura,* but whatever. She took a deep breath in the back lot, trying to settle herself down. She didn't know why she was so nervous—

Well, yes, she did.

And that reason was waiting for her out in front of the shop. He smiled when he saw her coming, and moved toward her out of the lengthening shadows. Cassie felt her breath leave her in a rush.

"You changed," Trey said. "I'm dressed like a scumbag, and you look gorgeous. How is that fair?"

"I thought I told you a long time ago," Cassie replied easily, thinking of the tiny pink crown. "I'm the queen." Inside, she thrilled to the word *gorgeous* and replayed it over and over again.

"I remember," Trey said, his voice warm and appreciative.

Side by side, they walked down the street toward Crescent Avenue, which was still bustling in the late afternoon shadows. An odd silence fell between them. Cassie sneaked a look over at Trey, and he met her gaze. She felt herself blush, but Trey only smiled.

"I thought we could grab something to eat," Trey said. He waved at his clothes. "Nowhere fancy, obviously."

Cassie thought his khaki shorts and T-shirt looked just fine beneath an open button-down, and she wasn't sure how he managed to look laid-back rather than prepped out, but he did. She'd never seen him not looking amazing, though. Maybe it was that twine around his neck. Or maybe she was just far too susceptible to him.

"You look fine," she said. "Are we going to a black tie gala?"

"We could probably swing that," Trey replied, laughing. "I'll just tell them I'm with the queen and I'm sure no one will give it a second thought."

"I like the way you think," Cassie told him.

Trey led Cassie down to Crescent Avenue and into one of the restaurants that overlooked the harbor. It was a restaurant Cassie had never been in before, though she'd walked past it a million times on her way to and from work. She liked that he was taking her to a place that was new to her—it made the fact that she was there, with Trey, feel more special somehow.

Don't get carried away, she told herself sternly as they were led to a table tucked away in the corner, with candles flickering and a sweet view of the evening bustle on Crescent and the boats bobbing on their moorings. *He wants you to think this is something special. It's just dinner.*

"So," Trey said, his fingers tapping lightly against the menu and his eyes on Cassie. "You're the queen, you give a great ride"—Cassie laughed despite herself at that, while Trey grinned—"and you can wear the hell out of a red dress. And, for some reason, you seem immune to my obvious charm. What's your deal?"

"What deal?" Cassie shrugged nonchalantly. "I'm here, aren't I?"

"That's it?" His smile could have melted Superman's ice castle in about a minute. Cassie pinched herself under the table to keep from squirming. "You're just going to sit there? You're not going to tell me even one thing about yourself?"

"I didn't realize there were so many rules," Cassie taunted him, watching his dark eyes brighten. "I thought we were just having dinner."

"You're cold and cruel," he told her. "What do you want to know about me? You can ask me anything."

Are you now, or have you ever been, a user of epic proportions? Cassie asked him in her mind, her eyes narrowing. Trey laughed.

"Uh-oh," he said. "Maybe I shouldn't have said that."

"I know about you," she replied mysteriously, hoping it would unnerve him. But she relented a second later. It was the way he was looking at her. Or maybe it was that smile he couldn't seem to get rid of no matter what she said. Maybe it was both. "Well, I can tell you about boarding school," she said. "It's kind of like summer camp and school at the same time."

"The good parts or the bad parts?" Trey asked, leaning forward.

"Exactly," Cassie said with a snort, and proceeded to tell him a few stories of some of her more outrageous antics. Like when she and a few of her friends had sneaked out of the girls' hall to go to a party with the senior boys, and yet only Cassie had gotten busted.

"Wait," Trey said at one point, laughing so hard he

actually wiped at his eyes. "You got caught sneaking *back in* to your dorm?"

"Laugh it up," Cassie replied dryly. "I didn't think it was so funny when I had to spend the next weekend scrubbing all the graffiti off the walls outside the gym. It was that or write my parents a long letter explaining my whereabouts that night." She shuddered. "My dad likes to think I'm Amish, so . . . graffiti it was."

"They made you choose?" Trey asked, shaking his head. "In my school it was automatic detention, no questions asked."

"Siskiyou is all about choices," Cassie said darkly. "They claim it builds character."

"I hope you learned a valuable lesson," Trey said, trying to keep a straight face.

"Sure I did," Cassie said, grinning at him. "I learned never again to sneak into my dorm after curfew, when I could have walked in with my key and claimed I was at the infirmary."

"I love the idea of boarding school," Trey told her. "I want to believe it's like Hogwarts or something."

"Except with a lot fewer wizards," Cassie said.

Trey laughed, but then he looked away. He shrugged. "I used to fantasize about going away to school," he said. "Things were kind of rocky with my parents for a while, and I guess I thought it was my fault. I figured if I went away, they could fight about something else."

Cassie felt as if she'd been socked in the gut. Trey looked so vulnerable, but that didn't make any sense with what she knew about him. Confused, she unfolded her napkin over her lap, and smoothed it carefully along her thighs. She wanted to reach across the table and hold on to him, but she shook that impulse off.

"Why would they fight about you?" she asked tentatively.

His gaze was troubled when he looked at her, and it made her breath hitch. He tilted his chin up. "I don't think they really were," he said. "I think they were just fighting, and I happened to be there." He smiled at Cassie's expression. "It's okay," he said. "Things were really tense a year or so ago. It's much better now."

He changed the subject, and soon was back to his usual teasing and flirting. Cassie couldn't help responding, but she wondered about what he'd told her. Had she finally seen the real Trey Carter?

After dinner, they walked down to the water and sat on a bench overlooking the harbor as night fell all around them. Cassie was full from too many cannolis and too much looking at Trey. Both were way too rich. Sinful, even.

"The stars are so bright here," Trey said, looking up. "It's never really dark enough at my house."

Cassie tipped her head back and looked up at the night sky, filled to bursting with stars. And when she looked out across the water, she could see the lights of the California mainland gleaming into the dark. It was all so beautiful that her chest ached a little bit—or maybe that was simply the fact that Trey was so close to her. She suspected it was both. She could feel him move next to her on the bench. She felt the brush of his arm, the scrape of his thigh against hers as he shifted position. She was afraid to look at him, afraid that it would mean more than she wanted it to. But then she dared to sneak a look and bit back a gasp of surprise because he was watching her.

His eyes seemed even darker in the night, and Cassie felt more than saw him move closer. She held her breath. He reached over and very gently, very carefully, pushed her hair back from her face.

"Cassie Morgan, you are trouble," Trey said softly.

"Said the pot to the kettle," she replied in a sassy sort of voice, one that made it seem like there was nothing but flirting and fun between them, and none of that vulnerability that she'd seen in him. Or suspected he could see in her.

"I'm not trouble at all," Trey protested, still so very close. "I'm just a guy trying to get a girl to give him the time of day. I'm like every song on the radio."

"Uh-huh." Cassie eased away from him and smiled. "Somehow, I'm not quite buying it. You don't strike me as the pure and innocent type."

"Pure and innocent, maybe not," Trey said, with a grin that made something warm uncoil inside Cassie. Then he looked serious. "But my intentions are good."

Cassie wanted to surrender. She wanted to lean in and press up against him and let the island magic wrap around her and become part of his magic too. She swayed toward him like he was some kind of snake charmer.

But then reality intruded, blowing its horn. Cassie gasped when she heard it, and jumped to her feet.

"The last ferry!" she cried, sudden visions of having to sleep on the floor of the bike shop—with Trey Carter—dancing through her head. "It's going to leave without us!"

"Let's go!" Trey leapt to his feet and grabbed hold of Cassie's hand.

He held her hand tight as they raced down Crescent Avenue toward the ferry landing, both of them laughing like loons and gasping for air as they went. Cassie's flip-flops slapped against the ground and her dress tangled with legs, but none of that bothered her—she felt like she could fly just then, if she wanted to—leap up into the Catalina hills and soar off toward the stars.

Finally, they skidded to a stop at the entrance to the ferry, only to be met by the cool stare of the *Catalina Express* crew member standing there.

Giggling uncontrollably, Cassie handed over her ticket. Assuming a grave expression, Trey did the same.

"You kids are lucky," the crew member said sternly. "We reserve the right to give away tickets less than fifteen minutes before departure. But no one was trying to ride standby tonight." He shook his head. "Welcome aboard."

Cassie was still laughing as Trey led her onto the ferry and to the upper deck, still holding her hand. He let go when they got to the outside seating area, and Cassie dug into her bag for her sweatshirt. Greta would faint from the horror of throwing a sweatshirt over a pretty dress, Cassie knew—but then, Greta was willing to be a lot colder than Cassie was. Once she'd zipped up her hoodie, she joined Trey near the railing. She looked over the side and back toward the village of Avalon and the bright lights from the dome at Casino Point. She could smell the salt and sting of the ocean, and when Trey moved closer to her, she could feel the warmth of him, flooding into her like he was some kind of walking space heater.

"Good thing you bundled up," Trey said approvingly as the ferry began to move. "It's going to get chilly up here."

Cassie turned toward him to say something—to continue the easy banter that had made the evening so much fun—but when she faced him, her words died in her throat.

His dark eyes were so intense that Cassie almost wanted to look away. Almost.

He reached over and slid his hand over the cap of her hair, as if memorizing the shape of her head. Then he stepped closer, pulled her toward him, and kissed her.

And Cassie wanted to die.

Or dance.

His mouth was warm and fit hers perfectly. He tasted like heaven. He slanted his mouth over hers, again and again, until Cassie thought she might faint. Then he pulled back and laughed slightly.

"I've been wanting to do that for a long time," he whispered. "I hope it's okay."

"It's more than okay," Cassie whispered back, and pulled him close again.

She'd kissed her share of other guys this summer— well, three of them, anyway. And none of them had made her feel like this, like she was made of champagne, all bubbles and giddy pleasure. Trey smiled against her mouth and wrapped his arms around her, holding her tight against his lean, muscled chest. She thought of Greta's warning briefly and then dismissed it, unable to imagine how a guy who had showed her his pain and then kissed like this could be anything but sincere.

Kissing Trey was the highlight of her summer. In fact, she thought as she snuggled closer to him and wound her hands around his neck, she could probably die happy right then and there.

But she kept kissing him, just to be sure.

Chapter Thirteen

✦

Cassie felt like doing cartwheels the next morning. She was still giddy from the night before and couldn't seem to wipe the goofy smile from her face. She was supposed to meet Greta and Keagan at their favorite brunch spot, Quality on Third Street, at 9:45 a.m. on the dot. Any later and the weekend lines would be too long—and all three of them, as L.A. natives, felt that they shouldn't have to wait in brunch lines.

But it took Cassie forever to get going. She kept staring off into space, remembering the way Trey's hands had felt against her face, or the heat of his mouth against hers. She was practically loony over this guy, she thought, laughing at herself when she realized she had been standing in the steamy bathroom with only her towel and wet hair, gazing dreamily into the distance, for way too long.

Somehow, Cassie managed to get her act together long enough to throw a bandana over her hair and slip on one of her favorite Anthropologie dresses. She stepped into her vintage Frye boots that she'd scored at a secondhand shop up on Melrose a few years back. Then she raced out the door, jumped in the car, and guiltily made it to Quality by ten.

"You're lucky we got a table already," Greta told her, making a face as Cassie slid into the seat they'd saved for her at one of the outside tables. "Check out the line!"

Cassie peered over her shoulder and sure enough, the brunch line had already tripled in size since she'd left her car with the valet. Los Angelenos took their brunches very seriously, especially on the weekends. Some people on line looked impatient or hungover. Others read the paper or chatted as the summer morning grew hotter.

"I think it had a lot more to do with the fact that we've known the people who work here for, like, a million years," Keagan interjected, around a yawn. "They usually don't let you hold a table until everyone's here."

"I know, I know," Cassie said apologetically. "I suck."

"Maybe you do and maybe you don't," Greta teased her. "But until I have coffee and a couple of biscuits, I don't think I'm going to care."

Cassie tried to keep her cool as the other girls chatted about what they'd done the previous night—though she kept breaking into that goofy smile, no matter how hard she tried to stop it. The smile she gave the guy who brought them their coffee and took their orders was so bright and beaming he looked a little taken back by it. *Oops,* Cassie thought, and stifled a giggle.

"I hate closing down the restaurant at night," Keagan was saying. "There's always some table that won't leave, and we have to stand around and pretend we think it's awesome that they're still sitting there talking about their kids or whatever, when really we want to just chase them out. And then it takes forever to clean up. Although it is kind of fun to hang out with everyone afterward. The other waiters are pretty cool."

"You totally made out with that guy again," Greta pronounced, eyeing Keagan over her mug of coffee, to which she added four packets of sweetener and half the little container of cream. Cassie sipped her latte, content to watch Greta go after Keagan. After all, she had too much Trey on the brain to contribute anything herself.

"I totally did," Keagan confessed, and shrugged, though she didn't look too guilty. "I couldn't help myself. He has these *shoulders,* you know?" She traced them in the air in front of her. "They're like the perfect boy shoulders, sculpted and touchable. I don't know."

"Making out with him again does not up your

numbers, K," Greta said, shaking her head as if disappointed in Keagan. "You could have been out kissing a new guy."

"I know, and I'm fully committed to the project, I promise," Keagan said, laughing. She wrinkled up her nose. "I just couldn't help myself. He's a *really* good kisser!"

Greta shifted in her seat, cupping her hands around her coffee. "I wish I could have been worrying about who to kiss last night," she said. "But I was stuck having family night."

"You always complain about it," Keagan pointed out, "but your family actually has fun on family night. Unlike in my house, where we just have dinner together when my mom reads something in one of her magazines that says we should eat as a family."

"Did you go to Hollywood Forever?" Cassie asked Greta, trying to pretend she was involved in the conversation, rather than a million miles away, still on the Catalina ferry in the dark with Trey.

"Maybe it's kind of fun," Greta admitted. "But it's also weird. How many families do you know who pack up a picnic and go hang out in a graveyard?"

"It's not like you were on a grave-robbing expedition," Cassie said, rolling her eyes. "I love the Hollywood Forever movie nights." Every summer, the Hollywood Forever cemetery in Hollywood hosted movie nights. They showed classic movies on the side of one of the buildings, and people came in droves to picnic and watch movies under the stars. Cassie thought of it as just one more quirky reason to love her hometown.

"I guess," Greta said noncommittally. "It would have been way more fun if there were cute boys involved."

"Like there were no cute boys there?" Keagan demanded. "I don't believe it!"

"There were a few," Greta admitted, grinning. "But it's not like I could do anything about it with my parents right there. Not to mention my little brother and sister."

"A wasted opportunity, Greta," Keagan teased her. "I'm ashamed of you."

"What is going on with you, Cassie?" Greta asked then, startling Cassie, whose attention had drifted once again. Cassie had the uncomfortable suspicion that there might have been a big gap in the conversation. Sure enough, both of her friends were staring at her.

"Um, nothing's going on," she said, stalling for time. Did she want to tell them about Trey?

"You lie," Keagan said breezily. "You've been acting super weird and distracted since you got here."

Cassie bit her lower lip, but the giddiness was too much for her. She still felt like jumping up and doing cartwheels down Third Street, and how could she not share that with her best friends?

"Okay," she said. "I'll tell you. But you have to listen to the whole story before you judge me."

"You know we love stories!" Keagan cried, looking delighted.

"And we won't judge you, silly," Greta chimed in. She raised her eyebrows. "Unless you deserve it."

So Cassie told them. She skipped over the earlier Trey sightings but told them how he'd showed up on Catalina and taken her to dinner. She told them all about how sweet he'd been, and what a great time they'd had. How easy things had been with him. She left out the stuff about his parents, because that was private. And she told them *most* of the juicy details.

"I know what you told me, Greta," Cassie said when she was finished with the story, "but he was totally sincere last night. I'm sure of it."

But when she looked over at Greta, her friend's expression had changed from its usual one of mischieivousness to something very serious. Keagan looked from Cassie to Greta and then back again, stricken.

"Oh, Cassie," Greta said with a heavy sigh. "I tried to warn you!"

"I know you did," Cassie said. "But I really think—"

"Let me tell *you* a little story," Greta interrupted, leaning forward, frowning. "Trey Carter is not a good guy, Cassie. I'm sorry, but he's not."

"I just can't believe that," Cassie said helplessly. She

felt terrible. She didn't want Greta to be mad or disappointed with her, but she'd been the one with Trey last night, and she hadn't seen even the faintest glimmer of player behavior. Quite the opposite, in fact. What was Greta's problem with him?

"Trey Carter sees girls as challenges," Greta said, her eyes cool. "Like little projects for him to practice on. Once he feels like he has a girl, he's out. He'll drop her." She blew out an angry breath. "Last year he promised to take this girl to the junior prom. But then she hooked up with him at a party the week before. She thought they were getting together. But Trey Carter, winner that he is, completely ditched her and took someone else instead."

Cassie could only stare at Greta as Keagan made a distressed sound from beside her.

"That is so low," Keagan murmured. "Greta told me this story last year when it happened. I'm sorry, Cassie, but it's awful. Still."

"And it wasn't like it was a mistake or misunderstanding or anything," Greta continued, her eyes on Cassie's face. "Everybody knew. He humiliated this girl, and when she asked him why he said, and I quote, 'Just because.'" She paused to let that sink in. "Just because. That's who he is."

Cassie rubbed her palms over her face, trying to make sense of what she was hearing. But it was almost too much to take in.

"You can ask anyone from my school," Greta said then, sitting back, still with that hard light in her eyes. "It's just a small part of the Trey Carter legend. I wish I could say it was a onetime thing, but it's not. That's how he treats girls. He gets off on it."

"I . . . I don't know what to say," Cassie managed to get out. Her head was spinning. The Trey she thought she knew could never have done something like that. But how well did she know him? Greta had gone to school with him for years. She had to know him better than Cassie did. Cassie felt like she might burst into tears. Or scream—anything to get the awful feeling out of her.

"Cassie," Greta said, her tone almost apologetic, "I wish I didn't have to tell you any of this. I wish he was the guy he pretended to be. But he's not. And what kind of friend would I be if I sat by and let him hurt you the way he's hurt so many other girls?"

"No," Cassie said, pushing the words out past the fog in her throat, "you did the right thing. I'm glad I know." Because it was better to know, wasn't it?

"I don't want to see it happen to you," Greta said.

Cassie was saved from answering when their food arrived—fragrant biscuits that were usually Cassie's favorite thing in the world, and fluffy omelets all around, all of it looking absolutely delicious.

But Cassie couldn't taste a thing.

Chapter Fourteen

◆

Somehow, Cassie wasn't surprised to see Trey the next morning on her ferry.

She'd ignored at least three phone calls and a million texts. She hadn't been able to deal. When she'd gotten home from brunch, she'd just shut herself in her room, listened to Band of Horses, and brooded. She might even have cried a little bit, which made her furious—because she shouldn't cry over someone as gross and calculating as Trey Carter apparently was. And because she had vowed not to get her heart involved, but look what had happened!

Cassie walked toward Trey, grimly noticing how casually hot he was. Like he was made to be looked at on the water, with the sun and sea all around him, so that his dark hair ruffled a little bit in the breeze. It was unfair that anyone was that easy on the eyes, and at the same time so evil.

"There's playing hard to get," Trey said when Cassie drew close, his tone light, but the look in his eyes anything but, "and then there's disappearing from the face of the earth. What happened to you?"

"I'm not playing hard to get," Cassie snapped. "I'm not *playing* at all."

"Okay." He studied her for a moment. "Then I guess I should assume your phone died?"

Cassie could give him the silent treatment, which maybe wasn't the most mature thing in the world, but so what? Why should she bother talking to him? He would probably lie. Except there was that part of her that wanted to hear his explanation for the story Greta had told. Because she so very much wanted to believe that he had an explanation—that there was a reason.

"Do you consider yourself a good guy?" she asked him, crossing her arms over her chest as the ferry began to move. She didn't sit down next to him. "Like, a good person?"

"Uh, sure," Trey said. He frowned in confusion. "What's going on?"

"So if I ask you something, will you answer me?" Cassie pressed him. "And do you promise to tell me the truth?"

"Of course," Trey said. He still sounded bewildered. "Anything you want to know." The early morning breeze whipped off the water while tourists in brightly colored windbreakers huddled inside the boat's cabin for warmth. But Cassie could only see Trey.

"Your junior prom," Cassie shot at him. "My best friend Greta told me a story about a girl you were supposed to take, who you then turned around and dumped the week before so you could go with someone else."

Secretly, Cassie hoped Trey would react with outrage—call it all lies, demand to know why Greta would something so nasty about him. But he sighed and looked away. Her stomach sank through the boat and into the water below. Part of her hadn't believed Greta, not fully, until that moment.

"So it's true?" Cassie demanded, scandalized. "You did that?"

"Okay," he said, looking back at her, his expression serious, "listen. It was a long time ago—"

"Who cares when it was?" Cassie felt heat and dampness behind her eyes and couldn't tell if it was from sadness or anger. But she refused to cry in front of him. "You're either the kind of guy who would do that to someone or you're not."

"I'm not!" Trey protested. He sighed. "But I was." Cassie snorted in disgust, and he hurried on. "I was an ass," he told her. "It was my junior year and I was completely full of myself. I was a starter on the lacrosse team and I thought I was hot. But then I got hurt in practice last fall, and I had to sit out the season. It sucked, but it also made me think a lot about how I'd been acting." He searched her face with his dark eyes, shifting his stance as the boat moved beneath him. "I changed, Cassie. I promise. I would never do something like that now. I don't know how I did it then."

"Why should I believe that?" Cassie whispered. "Isn't that what you *would* say?"

"I really like you," he told her, holding her gaze. "I care about you."

"I have no reason to think that's true," Cassie told him. Though she wanted to. Oh, how she wanted to.

"I know," he said. "But I couldn't fake how things are between us. Whatever else you know about me, you have to know that."

Cassie felt herself soften. Was she falling into his trap?

"I have to think," she said, feeling overwhelmed.

She walked away from him and went to sit in the cabin near the snack bar. Trey didn't follow her.

✦ ✦ ✦

It was late that evening when the ferry docked back on the mainland, and Cassie was pleasantly tired out from a long day at work. She'd led two separate tours, and then had taken an unexpected hike when one of the kids on her afternoon tour let his bike fall over the side of one of the hills. Cassie had had to climb down and drag it out, which had made her feel strong and in charge—which felt good after all the emotional turmoil of the morning.

But her heart did a little somersault in her chest when she looked up and saw Trey waiting for her in the parking lot, leaning against her car.

"Why are you here?" she called across the lot, though there was no sting in her voice. "Nothing's changed."

"That's what I was going to say." He straightened when she came closer, and pulled her into his arms. She didn't resist. The truth was, she didn't want to. "So you heard a story about me. It was true a long time ago, but it's not true now. And it has nothing to do with us."

"Trey . . ." But Cassie couldn't think of an argument. He felt so good against her body. It was like her skin and bones had made their own decision about him already and were fighting her to get closer to him.

"Come on, Cassie," he whispered. "I can't change the things I did. But I swear to you, I'll never do them to you."

Cassie sighed, and then somehow she moved, and she was kissing him. He tasted so good, like sugar and sunshine, and she didn't know how she could do without it. Without *him*.

But then she remembered her friends and groaned.

"I can't," she said. But she kissed him again. And then once more.

"Okay," Trey murmured, his hands holding her hips as he kissed her. "Except I kind of think you already are."

Cassie groaned again. "Seriously, I can't be with you," she said. "Or anyone."

Trey laughed against her mouth, and kissed her forehead. "Are you a nun all of a sudden?"

"My friends and I made a pact," Cassie said. "We decided to have . . ." She paused. He had a scandalous past of his own, but somehow, she didn't think he would like the sound of a ten-boy summer. Call it female intuition. "A single-girl summer," she said, deciding to be discreet about it. "They'll be really hurt if I bail on them. Especially—" She cut herself off again.

"Especially with me," Trey finished for her. He sighed a little bit. "It's okay, Cassie. I get it."

"It's just that they warned me about you," Cassie said, wanting him to understand. She peered up at him. "Specifically."

He sighed again and then shrugged. "So don't tell them," he said.

"I'm not going to lie to my friends!" Cassie replied. But something whispered that it would be a whole lot easier not to tell them. She frowned. "We can't have a secret thing, can we?"

"You need to figure out how to tell your friends," Trey said. "I get that. So take as much time as you need. Maybe you need to figure out how to trust me too." He ran his hands over her hair, and smiled down at her.

"Maybe I do," Cassie replied, unable to stop herself from smiling back at him.

"See?" He kissed her again, a long and lingering kiss. "We can do this. We can keep it to ourselves until you're ready."

"I'll tell them soon," Cassie promised, closing her eyes and arching into him. She felt alive and ridiculously happy, and felt only the slightest twinge of guilt at the secrecy. But she knew Greta would freak. She needed to come up with a plan—and didn't it count for something that Trey was so understanding? "I just need a little time."

Chapter Fifteen

✦

Cassie was out the door and down the front steps almost before Trey's car parked at the curb. It had been a week since he'd waited for her at her car, and this was their first official date—on the California mainland, anyway. For some reason that little fact had Cassie practically over the moon. It made it all so *real*, somehow. Like Catalina was this little bubble, and all the time they'd spent together over there was something out of a dream.

This was different. This wasn't dinner after work or a walk along Descanso Beach. It was a warm August night in the city, and this was really happening.

Trey climbed out of his car as Cassie approached, and as usual, Cassie's heart stuttered in her chest.

He was so gorgeous. Tonight he wore jeans and a blue button-down shirt with an embroidered pattern that managed somehow to emphasize his lean torso, narrow hips, and that confident way he held himself. His dark hair looked adorably ruffled, and the crooked smile he aimed at her made her breath come faster.

Cassie was glad she'd taken extra time with her appearance tonight. She'd figured that this was one of the few times that Trey would see her dressed up—instead of post-bike-tour Cassie, with windswept hair, too much sun, and only flip-flops. By this point she thought he'd probably forgotten how cute she'd looked at that first summer party. It seemed like that had been ages ago.

So she'd spent a long time in the shower, and then even longer blow-drying her hair. She'd made sure her makeup was perfect. She'd pulled on a pair of glossy black Bermuda shorts that she'd paired with very high, ankle-strap black shoes, and put on one of her favorite, dressiest tops: an off-the-shoulder silvery number from Miss Sixty that sparkled when she moved. She felt sleek and pretty, and the heat in Trey's eyes as she moved closer to him confirmed it.

"Hi," Cassie said softly. Speaking felt too intimate. He held out his hands, and Cassie loved the slide of his palms against hers.

"You look amazing," he said, his voice soft. It was like neither one of them could believe they were there together, with the whole night ahead of them and no ferry to worry about catching. After a moment, Trey ducked his head and nodded toward the car. "Come on," he said. "We should get going."

As he aimed the car north, toward the Hollywood Hills, Cassie relaxed in the passenger seat and tried to push away the sudden feeling of guilt that suffused her as her phone vibrated in her bag. It wasn't that she regretted being with Trey—because that wasn't possible—but she did regret having lied to Greta and Keagan about her plans for the evening.

Well. It hadn't been a *total* lie. There'd been a lot of texting about the night's activities, and Cassie had opted out of Keagan's plan for movie night and funnel cake at the Grove and the Farmer's Market at Third Street and Fairfax Avenue—one of her favorite places in the world. Cassie loved the outdoor fountain at the Grove, to say nothing of all the shops, and she really loved the eclectic mix of booths in the historic Farmer's Market. A movie at the Grove theater and then people watching with a lot of sugar? One of Cassie's top ten favorite L.A. nights.

But she'd told her friends that she needed a night off, and without actually saying it—or full-on lying—she'd hinted that she needed to get a good night's sleep for once. It didn't count as lying because she hadn't actually *said* that. Greta had said it; Cassie just hadn't corrected her. And then she'd told herself that she didn't feel guilty that she'd known it was safe for Trey to pick her up at her house because Greta and Keagan were safely off at the Grove. Not guilty at all.

Cassie pulled her phone out, biting her lip as she looked at it.

SURE U CAN'T WAKE YOURSELF UP? Keagan texted. GRETA HAS NEW PLAN. PIZZA + BOYS = CRAZINESS!! COME!

ALREADY IN BED, she texted back, another wave of guilt crashing through her, because there was no escaping the fact that she was lying now. Deliberately lying.

U R LAME, Greta replied. BOY BONANZA AT FARMER'S MARKET. LIKE HEAVEN!

HAVE FUN! Cassie texted. MY PILLOWS R PRETTY HEAVENLY!

Cassie shook the guilt off, because she'd made her choice and anyway, she wouldn't change it even if she could. Being so close to Trey made her whole body ache in a delicious way, and she couldn't stop smiling. How could she give up on that? Why would she want to—no matter what her friends thought of him?

"What are you smiling about?" Trey asked, looking over at her.

"This," Cassie said, deciding not to think about her friends anymore. Not tonight. She switched her phone off and tossed it back in her bag. "Didn't you say something about the perfect date?"

"I guess I did," Trey said. He turned toward her when he stopped at a red light, and there was the light of battle in his eyes. It made Cassie shiver in anticipation. "And one thing you should know about me, Cassie—I love a challenge."

✦ ✦ ✦

"The perfect date requires skill and planning," Trey told Cassie later, holding her hand as he led her through the crowd on Hollywood Boulevard.

Earlier, they'd swung by Pink's, the famous chili dog stand on La Brea. They'd laughed the whole time they'd stood on the equally famous line, which snaked around the back of the building and never seemed to get shorter—unless it was raining. After a wonderfully disgusting dinner of chili dogs with all the toppings, Cassie felt giddy and silly.

"The night is just beginning," Trey said. "Pink's was just a warm-up. You'd better get ready for extreme fun."

"Extreme fun better not mean, like, skydiving," Cassie told him, holding tight to his hand and loving the way her skin felt against his. "Because I think you're cute and whatever, but that doesn't mean I'm jumping out of a plane."

Trey's hand squeezed hers tighter, and he navigated a path around a man dressed as Superman who was shouting at another man dressed as Captain Jack Sparrow. Which was just par for the course on Hollywood Boulevard.

"You think I'm more than cute," he said, grinning down at her, his dark brown eyes gleaming. "Don't deny it."

"You're okay," Cassie deadpanned. But she shivered again, because the way he looked at her made her want to dance . . . or scream . . . or kiss him until she was reeling from it. Maybe all three at once.

"I would stop right now and demonstrate all the ways you think I'm more than cute," Trey informed her as he pulled her closer to his side, "but we're in a public place."

"That didn't stop you at Pink's," Cassie pointed out, smiling up at him.

"That was different," Trey protested. "I was eating chili dogs with a beautiful girl. That's like a male fantasy come true. How many girls can roll with a chili dog on a date? How could I not kiss you?"

It had been a great kiss, too—spicy and silly and still with that punch to the gut that Cassie was realizing was part of the Trey package. Cassie liked him more and more with every moment she spent in his company. Too much, maybe.

"Be careful of the guys in costume," she told him then, trying to keep it light. "I think they're stalking you."

Trey laughed and looked over his shoulder. Tourists swarmed the streets in front of the El Capitan Theatre and, across the boulevard, at the Hollywood & Highland complex. There were a million stores, Grauman's Chinese Theatre, and hundreds of people out roaming around in the warm summer night. Hollywood Boulevard was gritty and unreal, all at the same time, with homeless guys begging for change on the one hand, and people in superhero costumes mugging for pictures on the other. There were stars on the sidewalks and music blaring from the Virgin Megastore. It was chaos.

Cassie soaked it in, reveling in the mayhem of an ordinary August night on the boulevard.

Trey kept moving, across the intersection and then away from the main drag of Hollywood Boulevard. He kept walking until they hit a velvet rope, and then he grinned down at Cassie.

"I hope you're ready," he said. "I'm about to bowl you over."

He led her into a fancy, hipster-y bowling alley, which looked more like a nightclub, and which, Trey told her, required reservations.

"Bowl me over," Cassie repeated, rolling her eyes. "Ha-ha. For all you know, I'm the best bowler in California."

"Bring it on," Trey said at once, leaning in to kiss

Cassie on the forehead. "But first, I have a present for you."

He pulled a small package out of his pocket, and Cassie burst into laughter when she saw what it was: little white ankle socks.

"I thought you might be wearing cute shoes," Trey said, looking almost embarrassed suddenly.

"You thought about my shoes?" she teased him. And then she was sure—that was definitely a hint of red around his ears.

"Girls wear, you know, sandals or whatever," he said. They both looked down at Cassie's high wedges. "And I didn't want you to have to wear bowling shoes without socks, so I, uh—"

Cassie took pity on him, even as her heart swelled inside of her, and she felt that her smile might overpower her. She didn't think she could speak past the sudden lump in her throat, so she leaned in and kissed him. Once, sweetly, and then again, because one taste of him never seemed to be enough.

"Thank you," she said, and meant it more than maybe she should. But he'd thought about what *shoes* she might be wearing. That was adorable. And, to her mind, it proved that he really was the nice, caring guy he said he was. No matter who he might have been before.

Before didn't matter, Cassie thought, following Trey to the lane he'd reserved. Nothing mattered but that hopeful, happy look in his eyes—the one she knew she was wearing herself.

"You better get ready," she told him with all the bravado in the world as they sat down and put on their bowling shoes. Music blared from above, and Trey grinned at her.

"I'm ready." He leaned back, oozing confidence. "You can even go first if you want. Or take a handicap. Whatever you need."

"Keep being condescending," Cassie suggested, faking the tough talk and putting on a little swagger when she got to her feet. "It's only going to make this more fun."

✦ ✦ ✦

"Where are we going?" Cassie asked later, settling into the passenger seat of Trey's car. They'd bowled for a long time, finally calling the game a draw. Cassie was a little bit disappointed she hadn't completely dominated the game as she'd planned—but at least neither one of them had held back. They'd both been in it to win.

Trey was the first guy she'd ever played a game against who hadn't insulted her by acting like she wasn't up to his level, aside from the expected bit of teasing and trash-talking. It had been exciting to be able to compete with him without having to worry about hurting his ego or anything.

"I told you it's a secret," Trey said. He shot a look at her. "You'll just have to trust me, I guess."

"You really are cocky," Cassie teased him, thrilled when he reached over and took her hand again. She cradled it between her palms. She couldn't get enough of touching him.

"Confident," he corrected her, laughing. "Not cocky. There's a difference."

He drove up into Los Feliz, nestled at the base of the hills, and then turned up into Griffith Park. Cassie assumed they were headed to something at the Greek Theatre, and was surprised when he drove past the white building tucked away in the trees. There was only one other place to go.

"The Observatory?" she asked, delighted. "I didn't know you could drive up here again!"

"For a couple of years now," Trey said, as the car headed up the dark, winding road. "You really have been away, haven't you?"

They'd been renovating the iconic Los Angeles landmark for years. When it had opened again, people had had to make reservations on a shuttle bus in order to see the Observatory. It had completely killed the spontaneity of deciding in the middle of your evening to just drive on up to see the best view in the city.

"I love this place," Cassie breathed. "How did you know?"

"I didn't know." Trey looked over at her again, and his mouth kicked up in one corner. "But it's my favorite place in L.A. I hoped."

Cassie had to look away from him at that point, because she was afraid the swell of tenderness that overtook her would look like tears in her eyes. She felt shy suddenly, as if by taking her to this special place from her childhood, Trey had accessed parts of her no one else ever had. She felt vulnerable. Exposed.

But then he parked the car, and they got out into the night air, so cool up in the mountains, and Cassie forgot all that.

The Griffith Observatory sat high in the hills above Hollywood, with sweeping views of Los Angeles. Trey pulled Cassie close as they walked up toward the gleaming white building, lit up against the inky backdrop of the night. He draped one arm around her shoulders, and Cassie relaxed against him, surrounded by his warmth and the smell of his soap. They looked at the statue commemorating James Dean, and Cassie imagined that if she squinted, she could see Optimus Prime hanging off the side of the dome as he had in *Transformers*.

They climbed up to the roof and leaned over the side. Los Angeles expanded outward in every direction—threads of light knitted together into one huge, beautiful tapestry of reds and yellows and whites. The skyscrapers of downtown L.A. rose high and proud, but still couldn't approach the heights of the Observatory.

And up above all the messy lights of the city, the night sky was filled with stars, as if reflecting the city back upon itself. Cassie realized they hadn't spoken in a while, that they were both staring out at all the immensity and glow surrounding them.

"Kind of takes your breath away, doesn't it?" Trey asked, grinning at her and then looking back at the view.

But Cassie was looking at him. His face was dark against the bright lights below, but she could feel his warmth in the arm he pressed against her. She could feel *him* all around her. As if he'd created the view, and the perfect summer night, just for her. "Yeah," she said softly, "it really does take your breath away."

She knew, deep in her bones, that soon he would kiss her, and it would feel like it stretched on forever, beautiful and perfect, and like she could never, ever, be satisfied.

She could hardly wait.

Chapter Sixteen

◆

I can't believe I'm about to say this," Greta said from
beside Cassie, "but I think Keagan might be beating
me at Project Kiss, which is obviously unacceptable."

The girls were at a party down on the beach in
Venice. It was cooler by the water than it was inland,
especially after dark, and so everyone was rocking that
particularly Californian look, like a wool hat with flip-
flops, or a heavy sweatshirt over a bikini. Cassie was
somewhere in between, since she'd worn jeans and a fun
halter top that meant she was now shivering in the
ocean breezes. You'd never know it was the second week
of August.

"What do you mean?" she asked Greta, who, of
course, never paid any attention to the weather if it got

in the way of fashion, and was therefore wearing a dress that had probably started life as a tunic, that was how short it was. Needless to say, on Greta it looked fantastic.

"She was supposed to be getting us drinks," Greta said. "So, naturally, she is making out with Kenny Lawson."

Cassie snickered, and peered around Greta to see for herself. Sure enough, Keagan was all over some guy near the volleyball net—drinks clearly not foremost on her mind.

"No one can beat you," she said, turning back to Greta. "I mean, sure, K might get some numbers. But you're Greta. You're an institution."

"Flattery will get you everywhere," Greta said regally. "Please continue."

"Every guy here wants to make out with you, and every girl here hates you but secretly wants to *be* you," Cassie said, spreading her hands out to encompass the whole party and all of Venice beyond. "I'm not even exaggerating."

"You're so good for my ego," Greta said, sighing happily. She studied Cassie for a moment. "Something's different about you," she pronounced. Cassie felt a stab of fear—did Greta know about Trey? But then Greta grinned. "Clearly, coming home this summer was the right move. I think you needed it."

"I think you're right," Cassie said. Guilt and relief at not being caught mingled inside her and made her stomach hurt. She wished she were a better friend. She vowed to be, immediately. "I don't know what I was thinking, staying away for so long. Getting to spend all this time with you and K again has been amazing."

Greta blinked, surprised, and then her grin widened. "Well, yeah," she said. "Duh. We're the Three Musketeers, right? Except much, much hotter. And better dressed." She leaned close and pressed her shoulder against Cassie's, like a secret hug.

"If you can call that a dress," Cassie teased her, looking at Greta's outfit.

"Oh, you can," Greta all but purred. She eyed Cassie. "But what about you? Your fabulousness can't be overlooked."

"What?" Cassie pretended not to hear, striking a pose as she leaned closer. "Fabulous? What?"

"Totally fabulous in all ways," Greta declared, stepping back dramatically to look Cassie up and down, like she was judging *Project Runway*. "You have that laid-back but super-hot thing going on, which threatens all the girls, but they try to mimic it. And meanwhile the guys want to tell you their life stories"—she grinned wickedly—"and then stick their tongues down your throat."

"That's quite an image," Cassie said, making a face. She nodded across the sand toward Keagan, who was demonstrating the same image with her newest hookup. "You know that guy?" she asked.

"Sure," Greta said with a shrug. "Kenny's in my class. He's an okay guy. Not the brightest bulb, but who cares? He's pretty."

"You have to hand it to Keagan," Cassie said, with a surge of pride. "When she says she'll do something, she does it. One hundred percent commitment."

"She's making me feel like a slacker," Greta complained, and it seemed like she wasn't entirely kidding. "I feel like my reputation is at stake here. I'm only up to eight guys this summer! Keagan must have blown past that a while ago, don't you think?"

"I don't know," Cassie said, hedging, because Greta's "only eight" shocked her. "Only eight," when Cassie was still on number four. Number four, and not really interested in racking up any higher numbers. But how could she tell Greta that? "But that doesn't matter. You're an institution!"

"This institution is verging on tragedy, as far as I'm concerned," Greta said. She narrowed her eyes at Cassie. "But what about your numbers? The last was that guy at that party up in Laurel Canyon, right?"

"Ooh," Cassie cooed, in a desperate bid to change the subject. "Who is *that*?" She pointed toward the outskirts of the party, where a super-hot guy had just walked over to get himself a beer. He wore a ripped black T-shirt

that showed off two bright sleeves of tattoos on his muscled arms, and was doing fabulous things to the pair of
jeans he wore low-slung on his hips.

"Very Good Charlotte," Greta said approvingly. "I
can't believe you saw him first!"

"If you'll excuse me," Cassie said, grinning at her
friend, "I have some flirting to do."

Cassie made her way across the sand, happy to have
escaped the inquisition, but knowing it was temporary at
best. She needed to tell her friends what had happened.
That she and Trey had gone out despite Greta's warn-
ings. Repeatedly. Cassie only had to think of him and
she went warm all over. He was so funny, so sweet, and
so deliciously hot—why would she want some random
guy on the beach?

But she was a coward. She was afraid of what
Greta's reaction would be if—when!—she confessed.
Greta had a tendency to get really mad when people
didn't do what she thought they should. It wasn't like
Cassie was Greta's puppet or anything, but she'd
missed out on years of her friendship with her L.A.
girls while she was away at school. She didn't want to
give them any reason to think they were better off
without her around.

But she also didn't want Trey to think she was embarrassed to be with him or something. Not that he thought
that. Yet. Tonight he was hanging out with some of his

guy friends, but he kept texting her, just to say hello. Last night he'd picked her up after work and they'd ended up hooking up pretty intensely on the beach on Catalina. It made her knees feel weak, just remembering it. Cassie felt like he was a part of her somehow, even when he wasn't around—that was how much she missed him.

She knew Greta was watching her, so she made a beeline for Tattoo Guy.

"Hey," she said when she reached his side, smiling at him. "Want to get me a beer, while you're here?"

"Anything for a pretty girl," he replied at once, grinning back. His eyes traveled over Cassie's body, and he obviously liked what he saw. She was happy she'd worn the halter top, she decided, even if she was cold. He handed her an icy beer and moved closer while she opened it. "What's your name?"

Cassie figured she could compromise. Flirt with all the boys she could, so as not to make Greta and Keagan suspicious, but not *do* anything, so as not to feel slimy or like she was betraying Trey.

Only for a little while, she promised herself. *Just until I figure out how to break the news.*

"I'm Cassie," she told Tattoo Guy and, for fun, batted her eyelashes a little bit. Because if she wasn't going to *do* anything, the flirting was harmless.

And anyway, she was good at it.

✦ ✦ ✦

"You both are crazy!" Greta exclaimed much later, as the three of them walked the long blocks inland toward Greta's car, which they'd had to park a million miles away from the beach.

"Not crazy, just on a mission," Keagan replied at once. "Boys are fun."

"You're the make-out queen," Greta told her. "But Cassie! You were a superstar! Every time I looked up you were flirting with a different guy!"

"What can I tell you?" Cassie said breezily. "I'm very likeable, apparently." Except when she was lying, she thought, but she shoved it away. Cassie couldn't bring herself to tell her friends something that might make them treat her differently.

"When you wear a halter top and slink around like that, yeah, you are," Keagan said through a fit of giggles. "Check it out." She hunched over and started walking with a rolling-hipped gait that looked like a crabwalk, and then she stuck her chest out. "Look! I'm Cassie!"

"You're an idiot," Cassie retorted, swatting at her. "I'd show you what *you* look like, K, except I don't think Greta wants me slobbering all over her."

"I do not *slobber*," Keagan replied primly. "I kiss very delicately. And very well."

"I've created monsters!" Greta cried, which set them all off again.

Cassie linked her elbows with her friends, and the three of them careened down the sidewalk in Venice, making as much noise as possible and laughing into the night.

Chapter Seventeen

✦

When I die, I'd like to think heaven looks a lot like Robertson Boulevard," Greta said happily, propping up her hip against one of the tables in the trendy Kitson boutique. Cassie laughed and picked up another pair of jeans, which, while super cute, cost over eight hundred dollars. She studied them to see if she could figure out why. Extra-special embroidering, maybe? Or was it the fabric? It felt like normal denim to her.

Keagan was trying on a pair in one of the dressing rooms, to see what eight hundred dollars looked like when worn.

"I am totally serious," Greta continued, running her fingers almost lasciviously across a neat pile of T-shirts. "I live for this street."

They'd decided that their mutual day off was the perfect opportunity for a shopping extravaganza. Greta had insisted that they start off with lunch at the Newsroom, where healthy food was served up with all kinds of Hollywood industry people at the nearby tables. Then they'd lingered outside the Ivy for a little while, hoping that the scrum of paparazzi outside meant that someone really famous was having lunch there. Cassie's personal hope had been for Jake Gyllenhaal, while Keagan had been holding out for Zac Efron. Sadly, they'd seen no one they recognized. Greta had then insisted that they spend some quality time in Kitson— which she claimed was always the first stop on a Robertson shopping spree. Only after she'd gone through her beloved Kitson with a fine-tooth comb would she condescend to visit the other stores that lined the street.

"I look kind of fat in them," Keagan said, walking out of the changing booth with the super-expensive jeans over her arm. "For eight hundred dollars, I want to look in the mirror and see Keira Knightley, you know?"

"I hear that," Cassie agreed. She drifted over to another table, and picked up a vintage Team Jennifer T-shirt. "I lost mine," she said. "Do you think I should buy another?"

"You must be kidding," Keagan retorted, snatching the shirt out of her hand and picking up an artfully faded Team Angelina shirt instead. "Angelina and Brad are, like, totally sainted humanitarians with big hearts and so many cute babies, and anyway I can't forgive Jennifer Aniston for stealing John Mayer from me."

Cassie blinked. "Are you saying you like John Mayer?" She paused. "In public?"

"I can't help who I love," Keagan said seriously.

"This is not the summer of love, ladies," Greta scolded them. "It's the summer of boys. K, you must be up to like twenty by now." Cassie felt her shoulders tense up—her new and improved response every time Greta brought up Project Kiss. She told herself not to panic. She didn't have to lie or anything. She just didn't have to mention Trey. How hard could that be?

"Not *twenty*," Keagan said, grinning down at the display table. "I think I'm at nine."

"See?" Greta looked at Cassie. "I told you she was already winning!"

"We're not actually competing, are we?" Cassie asked, her voice dubious. "Like we're frat boys or something?"

"Says the girl in last place," Keagan scoffed. "Nice try, Cassie."

"What?" Cassie made a face. "Can I help it I'm a little more selective than you guys? I don't want to just trip and find myself making out with someone; I want to *choose* who to make out with. I want to own my experience." All of which was true. Cassie didn't mention that she'd become so selective that she'd picked one boy in particular.

"There was nothing in the Project Kiss pact about being *selective*, Cassie," Greta said, shaking her head. She and Keagan exchanged a look. "You're just trying to cover up the truth," Greta pronounced.

"What?" Cassie heard her voice squeak up. "I am? What do you mean?" How did Greta know?

"The sad truth is that you're at, what, five guys?" Greta continued with a laugh, obviously not recognizing Cassie's terror. Cassie made a vague sort of noise, which Greta obviously took as an affirmative. "And you've been super lame lately, with all the sudden wanting to *sleep*," Greta continued, teasing Cassie mercilessly. Cassie felt a deep pang of guilt. Because, of course, she hadn't been sleeping. She'd been with Trey. Part of her longed to be with him right now.

"You can sleep when school starts," Keagan chimed in. She ran her fingers over a display of hanging necklaces, making them dance. "I like to sleep in math class. Very restful."

Greta pointed a finger at Cassie. "There's a huge party in Silverlake this weekend," she said. "It will be overflowing with hot emo hipster boys."

"Emo hipsters?" Cassie echoed. "Not really my type, Greta."

"Hello, Cassie." Greta shook her head. "This is not

about your type, this is about boys to kiss. And hipsters are nothing if not kissable."

"That is actually *all* they are," Keagan said with a snort.

"Your numbers need to go up," Greta declared. "Not just for your own personal growth. But for all of us. This is about *girl power*, Cassie."

"Oh my God!" Keagan interrupted in a horrified voice—one that wasn't girl power-y at all. In the blink of an eye, Keagan went from lounging against the display table to hunched down on the floor, trying to hide *behind* the display table.

Cassie and Greta stared down at her. Cassie, to her shame, was grateful for the distraction.

"It's that guy!" Keagan hissed, frantically waving her hands toward the door.

"Sweetie, you need to be more specific," Greta said dryly.

"That football player guy from that party in the Palisades!" Keagan hissed.

Cassie had only a vague memory of the guy Keagan had hooked up with that night—since she had been far more taken up with meeting Trey and hearing Greta's crushing opinion of him. But when she looked over by the door, there was something familiar about the boy who stood there, all big shoulders and that football swagger. He was frowning in Keagan's direction.

Or, since Keagan was hiding, at Cassie and Greta. Greta sniffed and appeared unconcerned. Cassie felt her face go hot—almost as if the guy were glaring at her deliberately.

"Uh," Cassie said out of the side of her mouth, pretending to study the nearest pile of clothes, "I don't know how to break this to you, but I think he saw you. . . ."

Keagan swore under her breath and then peeked over the top of the table.

"He calls me like a thousand times a day," she whispered. "I have never responded, not once. I can't believe that in a city this big, I keep running into guys I don't want to see!"

"And . . . here he comes!" Greta singsonged.

"What do I do?" Keagan hissed, eyes wide.

"We'll create a distraction," Cassie said, apparently overtaken by Samurai Girl or something. "You just need to get around him and run for the door."

Greta looked over at Cassie and smiled, indicating that she was ready.

Cassie grinned back, and then it was like the two of them were in sync the way they'd been in that coffee shop with Zachary Malone. Football Shoulders marched across the store, glaring at Cassie, who looked back at him with a serene smile.

"Hey–" he began, but Greta "accidentally" tripped into him from her position near the hat display. She flopped against him, using all of her body weight to shove him off course.

"Eek!" Greta shrieked, as if she were onstage. "I'm so clumsy!"

"Sorry," the guy muttered, righting the both of them despite Greta's sudden attack of floppiness. When he finally stepped around Greta, his eyes scanning the area for Keagan, Cassie tipped over a display of books with a quick and dirty jolt from her hip.

"Hey! What are you doing?" one of the salesgirls shouted, as the books crashed to the floor all around Football Shoulders.

In the noise and confusion, Keagan bolted for the door.

Cassie and Greta looked at each other, then at the salesgirl bearing down on them with fury written across her face, and ran for it.

"If I get banned from Kitson, I'm killing both of you!" Greta cried when the three of them reunited outside the store, laughing.

"You spend way too much money in that store to get banned," Cassie assured her.

They all jumped when a voice boomed out from behind them.

"Keagan?" the guy asked loudly from a ways down the sidewalk. "Why won't you return any of my calls?"

The three girls all grabbed each other. Cassie didn't

know if she wanted to shriek or scream with laughter—
maybe both.

"Um, hi . . . ?" Keagan said weakly. Her eyes widened
in panic. "What am I supposed to do?" she hissed in an
undertone.

"You *did* spend the whole night making out with
him," Greta drawled. "I'm sure he feels you have a con-
nection—"

"Greta!" Keagan cut her off.

"You're doing fine," Greta murmured.

"It's me, Mark," Football Shoulders continued, moving toward them. "I met you at that party—"

"Sure," Keagan said, backing up—and right into
Cassie. She grabbed Cassie's hands and squeezed. "That
party."

"I keep leaving you messages," Football Shoulders
said, frowning. "Like a million since I last saw you."

"Maybe it's the wrong—" Keagan started to say.

"It's your voice," Football Shoulders insisted. "I
know your voice and, hello, your name is kind of
unusual."

"Um, you know, I have a thing about technology . . ."
Keagan rambled, clearly grasping at straws and at a loss.
She threw a pleading look at Greta—who was, after all,
the master when it came to uncomfortable guy situa-
tions.

"Keagan!" Greta said suddenly. "Your appointment!"

"My appointment? Yes!" Keagan cried, catching on. "My appointment."

"She has an appointment, uh, Mark," Cassie told the guy, who was scowling at them. "You know. So."

Very calmly, Greta turned around and started walking away. Not nearly as calmly, Cassie and Keagan followed her lead. But then they all glanced at one another and that was that—they all started convulsing with laughter.

Cassie glanced over her shoulder.

"You guys!" she hissed, though she could barely speak through the laughter. "He's following us!"

It only made them laugh harder.

And then there was nothing to do but run—up the street and past the pack of photographers who camped out in front of the Ivy, until they dashed across traffic and hid around the corner of the Starbucks, where they could track the approach of Football Shoulders Mark through the coffee shop's glass windows.

"I hope he gives up," Cassie said, clutching her sides where they ached from all the laughing. "I really want a mochaccino."

Keagan grinned at her and then kissed her loudly on the cheek.

"And that's why I love you," she said. "Always so practical!"

Chapter Eighteen

◆

The third time her phone buzzed in her pocket, Cassie ignored it.

"Do you need to get that?" Trey asked, breaking their long kiss and grinning down at her. He was leaning back against the counter in his parents' kitchen, with Cassie pulled up against him. They hadn't made it too far once she'd come in the back door. Cassie was just happy his parents were out for the evening at some fancy law gala, and therefore not likely to suddenly burst in on them.

"I'm good," Cassie told him, and then pulled his head back toward hers, feeling anxious to kiss him more. The more they kissed, the more she wanted to kiss him. Nothing was enough. He was addictive.

"You're sure?" He was teasing her now. He laughed

down at her scowl. "You answered the last two times. You can answer now, if you want."

"I don't want," Cassie said. She let out a noise that was half a sigh, half a groan, and all frustration. "But apparently, you do!"

Trey laughed again, and kissed Cassie on her forehead, then set her away from him. He eased away from the counter and headed across the kitchen toward the refrigerator.

"I just want your full attention," he said over his shoulder. "So if you have to text, do it now. That's all." He grinned back at her. "Unless you'd rather be somewhere else."

"I told you, I don't want to go out tonight," Cassie said. She pulled her phone out of her pocket, and waved it at him. "See? I'm turning it off."

Trey watched her as she turned her phone off and then set it down on the table with a little flourish. Then he gave her a smile that made her feel wobbly all through her body.

"As a reward," he said, "I think I'll make you my world-famous cheeseburger."

"You cook?" Cassie asked, and she couldn't help herself—she laughed. "When you said there would be dinner, I thought you meant, like, pizza."

"I can make a cheeseburger to die for," Trey said. "I watch a lot of *Top Chef*, you know. Oh ye of little faith."

"Are you sure?" Cassie asked. "I watch a lot of TV too, which is why I'm a big believer in pizza delivery."

"Cassie," Trey said, shaking his head at her, "I'm offering to make you a cheeseburger that's so mouth-watering it will change your life with one bite. And you keep talking about pizza delivery."

"I like pizza," Cassie replied, making a face at him. "I'm not really into E. coli."

"E. coli. Wow." Trey advanced on her, making her giggle. "So now you think I might poison you?"

"You just don't strike me as the cooking type," Cassie said, laughing harder when he grabbed her and yanked her closer to him.

"Keep it up," he said, eyeing her. But he was grinning when he planted a kiss on her mouth, fast and quick and still dizzying. "That kind of attitude leads to no dessert, that's all I'm saying."

Cassie laughed again and settled back against the kitchen counter, content to watch him pull ingredients out of the big Sub-Zero refrigerator and stack them on the counter. She loved the way he moved. She loved the sleek lines of his body, and the way wore his jeans slung low on his hips. She loved the fact that he was wearing an old, beat-up Stanford T-shirt that she suspected had once belonged to his father—and that it was so old it clung to his body and made her breathless. But most of all she loved how easy everything felt when she was with him.

She told herself she didn't feel guilty at all that she was blowing off the girls again. Greta and Keagan were headed out to that party in Silverlake, but Cassie had gone straight to Trey's house after work. She'd thought that maybe she'd meet up with them later—but once she'd seen Trey, she couldn't bring herself to leave again. First she'd claimed that there was bad traffic. Then she'd made some noise about being tired, too, and not sure she could motivate to go out. She'd been saved from any further lies by Trey's making fun of her—since she kept interrupting their kisses to respond.

The real truth was, she felt guilty because she *didn't* feel guilty about skipping the party. She didn't want to go. She wanted to wave a magic wand and have Greta and Keagan know all about Trey—and have them somehow be perfectly okay with her relationship with him. And then she wanted to sink into him and stay there for a while, without having to worry about keeping secrets or protecting feelings or anything else.

Soon, she promised herself. She would tell them soon.

✦ ✦ ✦

"I want a full apology," Trey said later, as they lay cuddled together out on the patio that ringed his pool. Cassie was full and happy and couldn't think of anything she'd rather do than be with him, within kissing distance. "Maybe even in writing. Assuming the E. coli doesn't get you."

"It was a good cheeseburger," Cassie admitted. "But we don't know the incubation period for E. coli, so let's not get carried away."

"Carried away? You fully doubted me!" He grabbed his chest, mock-wounded by her doubts.

"I only *sort of* doubted you," she replied, leaning closer and kissing him on his sexy mouth. The kiss was far more delicious than any cheeseburger, even a life-altering one.

Trey gazed down at her, and as Cassie looked back at him, she felt her heart swell. There was a heat behind her eyes, almost as if she wanted to cry, though she couldn't remember being happier.

"Sort of doubting me is still doubting me," Trey said softly, tracing patterns along Cassie's jaw and playing with her hair. "The goal here is to have no doubts."

Cassie knew he was talking about more than his cheeseburger prowess. She lifted her hand and let her knuckles smooth across his jaw. She loved the way his skin felt against hers. So warm, and then he turned his head and pressed a kiss to her hand, and she felt her breath catch in her throat.

"I doubted the cheeseburger," she said, whispering for some reason. "But nothing else. Everything else is doubt-free."

"Is that true?" He was whispering too. As he smiled down at her, Cassie would have challenged even Greta to question how true his feelings were. Cassie could feel an echo in her own body, shaking her.

She'd never felt like this before. She thought of Daniel Fletcher suddenly and wanted to laugh. She'd thought she was so desperately in love with him, but it had never been like this. She'd always been so . . . *afraid.* Afraid to tell him what she thought, or how she felt. Afraid that he wasn't interested in her, or that he would think she was silly, or too young, or not good enough. Always afraid. But with Trey, she was never afraid. She said whatever was on her mind. She laughed all the time—instead of stressing out that she wasn't smart enough or pretty enough for him. It was revolutionary.

"It's true," she told him. And she knew it was. She didn't care what Greta said, what Trey had done in his past. She believed him.

"I love you," he said, and then let out a kind of surprised breath, like he'd startled himself. Cassie froze. He smiled, and framed her face with his hands. "I'm in love with you," he said, more deliberately this time, like it had slipped out the first time and he wanted to get it right.

And suddenly Cassie knew.

That's what all these feelings were. Why she couldn't stay away from him, why she wanted to cry but wasn't sad—all of it. She'd thought love was painful and agonizing and all about *not good enough*. But it was about fitting so well with someone that everything felt bright and crisp and right.

"I love you too," she whispered, smiling so hard she thought her face might crack in two.

"Yeah?" he asked, smiling back at her.

"Yeah," she said.

Trey kissed her then, rolling over so the length of his body was pressing Cassie back into the chaise. She loved it. It was like a fire ignited between them, and she couldn't get enough of him. She helped Trey pull off his shirt. It was almost too much to be that close to him, to all that smooth, muscled skin—and then it wasn't enough. Cassie sat up and pulled her own shirt off, and they both sighed happily. When he pulled away from her, Cassie pulled him back.

"Don't stop," she whispered. "I want you to be the one."

"You want me to . . . ?" His eyes widened as he looked at her, as he got what she meant. "Are you sure?"

"I've never been more sure of anything," Cassie told him, and to prove it she stood and held out a hand. Trey blew out a breath, and Cassie felt a moment of panic. But then his smile kicked in at the corner of his mouth, so sexy, and his dark eyes moved over her like he'd never seen anything so beautiful. He stood too, and took her hand in both of his as he led her into his bed-room.

"Don't worry," he told her, smoothing his hands down her body, never looking away from her. "I'll take care of you. I promise."

And he did.

Chapter Nineteen

✦

The next night, Cassie was having trouble keeping her feet on the ground, when all she really wanted to do was float around somewhere in the stratosphere.

It didn't help that Trey was at the party Greta had dragged them to in the hills of Echo Park. He kept looking over at Cassie from where he stood with some friends, and the look in his eyes made her squirm. She wished they could go off somewhere alone—but that wasn't going to happen, not until she confessed everything.

Which she wanted to do, but she was so giddy from what had happened the night before that she didn't want to let anything potentially negative touch it. She wanted to float in the giddiness for a while.

The knowing look Trey gave her then made her flush. He was far too sexy for his own good. She sighed to herself.

"Earth to Cassie!" Keagan cried, and snapped her fingers in front of Cassie's face. Cassie focused on her and forced a smile. "You are so out of it tonight," Keagan continued, shaking her head. "What is going on with you lately?"

She glanced around, distracted from Cassie's flakiness by the prospect of a hot guy, and Cassie risked looking over in Trey's direction. Luckily, he and his buddies had turned away and were headed back inside the small house that commanded an impressive view. Cassie leaned back against the railing of the large sun-bleached deck that looked out from the hillside and told herself that she wasn't being a coward to keep the Trey secret just a little bit longer. She was holding on to something wonderful and private. She didn't want to have to defend it.

"There you are," Greta said, shimmying her way through a tight clutch of people, holding three beers in her hands. "Getting drinks was crazy. There are way too many people here, and *way* too many ironic sideburns."

"At least we got this one out of the house," Keagan said, nodding at Cassie.

"Seriously." Greta handed out the beers and then eyed Cassie. "What's going on with you?"

"Why are you guys all over me tonight?" Cassie asked

with a laugh. "Sometimes I get tired. It's no big thing." She hoped that had come off casual and easy, but Greta was watching her with a slight frown.

"I still think you're bailing on Project Kiss," Keagan said. She pointed a finger at Cassie. "And I know for a fact you didn't kiss that guy with all the tattoos down on the beach in Venice that time."

"What?" Cassie stalled for time, needing a moment to even remember the tattooed guy, or the party in Venice.

"We ran into him last night," Greta said, her eyebrows arching up. "Keagan told him she couldn't kiss him because you had." She paused and tilted her beer toward Cassie. "But he said he'd never touched you."

"Too bad," Keagan said with a giggle. "Because he's a really good kisser."

"When did I say I kissed him?" Cassie asked, trying to remain calm. It wasn't easy when Greta was looking at her so suspiciously.

"I was counting him in your tally," Greta said. "If he's not on the list, who is?"

"Wow, you guys are suspicious," Cassie said, trying to laugh it off. "I was never counting him in the first place."

"You're dragging your feet, missy," Keagan said, mock-accusingly. "You make excuses to not come out anymore. You don't kiss guys who, let's face it, are easily kissed."

"We all swore," Greta chimed in. "We made a pact. If you aren't into it anymore . . ." She let that sentence trail off, and shrugged.

Now, obviously, was the time to come clean. But Cassie opened her mouth and found she couldn't do it. Keagan and Greta were suspicious, but they were still teasing. Bringing up Trey would ruin that.

"I know we made a pact," Cassie said, making a big show of rolling her eyes. "Hello. I was there."

"You're obviously working too hard," Keagan said lazily, taking a swig of her beer. "If you have to sleep so much. There are only a few weeks left before school starts, you know. I think you're going to have to rethink your priorities."

"You mean, pay more attention to kissing and less attention to my summer job?" Cassie asked, laughing.

"Exactly." Keagan sighed. "You're way too responsible."

"Unless you're over the whole kissing thing," Greta murmured.

"Greta, please," Cassie said, rolling her eyes. "I'm all about kissing. I'm just picky. Didn't we talk about this?"

"You make a lot of claims," Greta said, "but I'm not sure anything happens."

"She's totally calling you out," Keagan said, taunting Cassie gently. "She's questioning your kissing skills, Cassie. Are you going to stand for that?"

Cassie could hear the laughter in Keagan's voice, but she was looking at Greta.

"You talk the talk," Greta said quietly, her hazel eyes narrowed. "But I'm not sure you walk the walk." And suddenly, it didn't really feel like teasing anymore. Maybe it was because Cassie knew she was lying to them, but this all felt too sharp. Cassie hated that Greta was looking at her like she didn't believe her, like she'd let her down. She knew that if she told the truth, Greta would be even angrier, and Keagan would stop teasing her and get serious. But she didn't know how to keep lying to them, either.

"Fine," Cassie said, shrugging as if she didn't care. "Believe what you want."

"How many guys *have* you kissed?" Keagan asked.

And it was the last straw.

"God," Cassie groaned. "You never give up, do you?"

She didn't know what she meant to do. She slapped her beer down on the dark wooden railing and looked around a little wildly. She caught Greta's smirk—like she knew she'd pushed Cassie—and Keagan's raised eyebrows. She just didn't want them to be angry with her. That was all. That was why she let her eyes fall on the nearest guy, a nice enough–looking boy in an Ed Hardy T-shirt. She marched over, interrupted his conversation, slid a hand around his neck, and kissed him. Not just a peck, either. She made it good.

She turned back to her friends and glared at Greta and then Keagan in turn.

"Satisfied?" she asked.

But then she saw Trey standing a little bit farther away on the deck, staring at her.

Cassie's heart dropped to her shoes.

"I'm totally satisfied—" Keagan was saying, but Cassie ignored her.

Trey.

She forgot about the secrets she was supposed to be keeping, and about what her friends might think. All she could see was that awful, hurt look in his eyes. She ran over to him.

"What the hell, Cassie?" His lips barely moved. She'd never heard him sound so pissed off before.

"I was just proving a point," Cassie said, wishing as she said it that it sounded a little bit better. "It didn't mean anything."

"That's how you prove points?" he asked sarcastically. "Wow."

"Don't look at me like that," she said. "You know I—" She couldn't say it, not when he looked so furious. Like she was a stranger.

"I can't believe I've been tiptoeing around trying to make up for stuff that happened years ago," he said bitterly. "And you're using your girl power summer crap as some excuse to hook up with whomever you want!"

"I am not," she said desperately. "I would never—"

He shook his head as if to clear it and stepped back. "Is this why you wanted to keep everything a secret?"

"No!" She was dimly aware that her voice was too loud, but she didn't care. All she could see was how mad he was, and how disgusted he looked. With her.

"Who's the player here, Cassie?" he hissed at her.

And then he broke her heart by storming away from her.

Cassie took a deep, shuddering breath. She could not fall apart in front of everybody. She couldn't let herself—

She turned and saw that Greta and Keagan were standing right there—and, from the looks on their faces, had heard everything.

Great.

"Are you kidding me?" Greta snapped. There were two spots of color high on her cheeks. "Trey Carter? After everything I told you?"

Cassie could no longer hold back the tears.

"I'm sorry—" she started, but Greta threw her hands in the air as if she could physically stop the words.

"I'm out of here," she snapped, and then she too stalked away.

Cassie had to stand there on the deck, surrounded by staring strangers and with Keagan's shocked expression front and center, wondering how her amazing summer had fallen apart so fast.

Chapter Twenty

✦

Cassie took a deep breath, blew it out, and then pushed open Greta's bedroom door.

She'd felt like such a fraud when Greta's mother had opened the door, welcoming Cassie and Keagan as if Greta had never stormed away from that party earlier that night. But Cassie had headed upstairs to Greta's room anyway, knowing that it was the right thing to do, no matter how much she wanted to fast-forward through this part. She didn't want to face Greta's anger— she'd been avoiding it all summer—but she knew she had to if she ever wanted to fix things with Trey.

Keagan was right on her heels, so Cassie had no choice but to walk through the door. Greta was standing over in the corner of her room, the contents of her closet spread out around her in a semicircle. Her eyes flew to Cassie's, and Cassie winced when she saw her friend had been crying. Greta's mouth tightened.

"What are you doing?" Keagan asked, easing around Cassie and walking over to perch on the edge of Greta's bed.

"I am organizing my closet," Greta said, very matter-of-factly. Almost defiantly.

"You sure are," Keagan said softly, staring at the jumble of shoes and mostly dark-colored clothes.

Cassie's guilt intensified. When they were kids and Greta's grandmother had died, Cassie had found Greta organizing her mother's kitchen cabinets an hour after returning from the funeral. But that had been a long time ago, and it had been the only time Cassie had ever seen Greta cry before now.

"Greta," she said, "I can explain."

"You can explain," Greta repeated. Her throat worked a little bit. "You don't have to explain, Cassie. I get it. All that 'catching up on your sleep'—you were lying. You were sneaking around with Trey Carter." Her voice cracked.

"I didn't know how to tell you," Cassie admitted. She could feel Keagan's gaze on her too, and wanted to sink into the floor. She would have given anything in that moment to disappear.

"God, Cassie," Keagan murmured, obviously also

disgusted with Cassie. Cassie couldn't believe how awful she felt. She kept on feeling worse too, no matter how often she thought, *This is it—this is the absolute worst I could feel.*

"How could you?" Greta demanded, her composure finally cracking. "How could you get together with him?"

Cassie shrugged awkwardly, feeling the tears prick at her eyes. She couldn't tell Greta what it had been like. That she loved him and even now wanted to run out and find him and figure out a way to make everything okay. That it was less *how could she* and more *how couldn't she,* and how none of it mattered anyway because of that horrible look in Trey's eyes when he'd walked away from her.

"It just happened," she said instead. "I know what you told me—"

"He's a bad person!" Greta shouted at her. "How many times do I have to tell you? Why would you go out of your way to get with someone like that? I'm the one who's known him for years, Cassie. You've known him for what? A couple of months?"

"Greta—"

"I don't know what's worse," Greta continued, and her chin trembled, though Cassie could see she was fighting back tears. "That you completely ignored what I told you, or that you decided you had to lie about it.

The old Cassie would never have done something like this!"

Cassie sucked in a breath, knowing Greta was right. But the old Cassie also wouldn't have dared to do half the things she'd done this summer. So how could she wish New Cassie away? And how could she tell Greta that New Cassie was just Cassie's version of Greta, anyway?

"You shouldn't have lied," Keagan chimed in then, still in that low murmur. "That's never okay."

"I didn't know what to do," Cassie said after a moment. "You were so sure that Trey was this awful guy—"

"Because he is!" Greta cried. "Do you think I just said that to be funny? Or did you think I was just randomly begrudging you a perfectly good hookup? He's a user! He'll tell you anything you want to hear to get what he wants and then when he does, he's gone."

"He's different now," Cassie said, feeling confused. She wanted to make things better with Greta, but she also felt like she had to defend Trey, even if he never spoke to her again.

"Guys like that don't change," Greta said bitterly. "They just learn how to hide it better."

"I asked him about it, Greta," Cassie told her, trying not to get angry, though she could hear the edge in her voice. "It's not like I didn't listen to you. I asked him about his junior prom."

Greta gaped at her for a moment. Then her arms crept around her torso, like she was hugging herself.

"Oh yeah?" she asked, her voice clouded with sudden emotion. "And what did he say?"

"He said he was a jerk back then, but sitting out his last season of lacrosse made him rethink a lot of stuff," Cassie said, ignoring her instinct to protect Trey's secrets. Cassie thought maybe if she gave Greta all the information, Greta would revise her opinion.

"I can't believe you would fall for something like that," Greta snapped. "He's a liar. And he's made you one too!"

"Okay, enough," Cassie said, her temper kicking in. "I shouldn't have lied to you. I didn't want you to be disappointed in me. But I don't understand why you're so anti-Trey."

"Because he's disgusting!" Greta cried. "Which you would see if you weren't completely under his spell like everyone else!"

"No, he is not," Cassie retorted. "You don't know him, Greta. Not like I do—"

"It was me." Greta interrupted Cassie in a ragged voice, and then her face crumpled. "I was the girl he was supposed to go to the prom with. It wasn't some random story I heard. *It was me.*"

Keagan sucked in a loud breath. "Greta!" she whispered. "Why didn't you tell me?"

Cassie couldn't move. She couldn't look over to see Keagan's shock. She couldn't seem to do anything but stand there, frozen in place. Her heart sank toward the floor. She felt hot, then cold, then hot again.

And suddenly everything made horrible sense. Why Greta had been so violently opposed to Trey. Why Trey had continued to pursue Cassie even when she was ignoring him—he'd already known what things Cassie might possibly have been hearing about him. Why Trey had so easily agreed to keeping things secret, and why he hadn't minded that Cassie might have to work to trust him—something that, in retrospect, other guys might have gotten upset about.

"Why didn't you just tell me that?" Cassie asked when she was sure she could speak without her voice cracking. "I would never . . . Why didn't you say it was you?"

"Why would you keep a secret like that?" Keagan chimed in, her voice troubled. "You told me the story when it happened. Why lie about who the girl was?"

"I don't know." Greta was still hugging herself. Tears flowed freely down her cheeks, and she made no move to wipe them away. "It's like I can't let myself think about it that way. And I didn't want you to know what a loser I was back then. He humiliated me."

"Greta . . ." But Cassie didn't know what to say. She didn't know what to think. She could kind of see why

Greta hadn't wanted to say that it was her, because the whole story was at complete odds with the tough, confident image she projected. In fact, Cassie had a hard time believing that Greta could be this hurt, all this time later.

But she was crying. *Greta* was crying.

"I believed him," Greta said. She wiped at her eyes finally, her hands balled into fists. "I believed everything he said to me. And after he humiliated me, I knew I'd never let anyone hurt me like that again. Ever. I can't bear to watch him do the same thing to you."

"Greta—" Cassie began again, but Greta held up her hands.

"I can't do this," she said. "I can't. Please." She looked over at Keagan, still sitting there on the bed with her eyes wide. Then she looked back at Cassie and her eyes filled up again. "I just want to be alone."

Cassie moved toward the door, Keagan beside her, not wanting to leave Greta like this but not knowing what else to do. Cassie looked back over her shoulder when she got to the door, and wasn't surprised to see Greta staring after her.

"I'm sorry he hurt you," Cassie said softly. She swallowed. "I'm sorry I did too."

Chapter Twenty-one

◆

When Cassie woke up the next morning, the first thing she did was roll over and check her phone. But there were no messages from Trey.

She collapsed back against her pillows and hated herself. She was such a terrible friend that, even now, Trey was her first thought instead of Greta. Cassie groaned out loud and then pulled herself out of bed. It was already past ten thirty, but even the extra sleep and the fact it was her day off didn't help her mood. She dragged herself into the shower, then downstairs to the kitchen. Her parents were both at work and Cassie had the house to herself.

Yay.

She dragged a box of Cap'n Crunch down from the

cabinet and took it with her to the couch in the family room, where she curled up in a ball, shoved the sugary cereal into her mouth, and tried to pretend she was fine.

But she gave up after a round of channel surfing, when the Cap'n Crunch was starting to cut up the roof of her mouth. And then there was nothing to do but think about the disaster her summer had become. Maybe it was a good thing that it was almost over.

Cassie couldn't believe how badly Trey had hurt Greta—and how badly *she* had hurt Greta. It was one thing for Trey to tell Cassie that he wasn't the jerk he'd once been, but Greta was the one he'd been a jerk to. Greta. Not some nameless, faceless girl whom Cassie never had to see cry. No wonder Trey hadn't mentioned any of that. Cassie would never date someone who had been with one of her friends. That was just icky. And someone who had broken her friend's heart? No. Way.

Cassie knew that she'd hurt Trey too, which made her feel even worse about herself. How had that happened? How had she managed to hurt everyone, all by trying not to disappoint anyone? Her mother always said that honesty was the best policy, quoting that cliché over and over again like she wanted to embroider it on a pillow or something, but now Cassie could see the wisdom of it.

If she'd only been completely honest from the beginning, none of this would have happened. If she had admitted her feelings to Greta, she would have heard the whole Trey story. She wouldn't have let Trey convince her to go out with him, so she would never have fallen in love with him. He would never have fallen in love with her. So no one would have been hurt when Cassie kissed that guy last night. And with all of that averted, Cassie never would have lied to her friends.

Cassie stretched her legs out along the couch and switched the TV over to HBO, but she couldn't concentrate on reruns of movies she'd been bored with years ago.

Cassie knew then that she had to face the truth. She might have hurt Trey by kissing that guy, but it was obvious from Greta's story that he would have hurt her eventually anyway. She believed that he'd changed, but how much? Not enough to tell her that Greta was the girl he'd hurt back before his junior prom. Not enough to tell her the one thing that would have made her think twice about getting together with him. So how far off the mark was Greta about him after all?

Greta had been there for Cassie since they were little kids. This summer was supposed to be all about the three of them breathing life back into their old friendship. And Cassie knew that they'd done all that—until Trey got involved.

Not that Cassie could blame it all on Trey. She'd been the one to lie and sneak around. She'd been the one to totally wimp out on telling her friends about him, because she knew they wouldn't like it. Greta had said something about Trey making Cassie lie, but the sad truth was that Cassie knew he'd had nothing to do with that.

That had been one hundred percent Cassie's choice.

Not very girl power-y of her. In fact, it kind of made her feel sick to think about. She'd wanted to be strong like Greta, but she'd been too chicken to do the truly strong thing and tell the truth.

Cassie got up, brushing Cap'n Crunch dust off her lap and telling herself it was time to stop moping. Summer was almost over anyway. She'd made a lot of mistakes, but she didn't have to keep making them.

Starting right now, she could grow up.

✦ ✦ ✦

Cassie found Greta up in her room again. This time, Greta was lying across her bed when Cassie walked in, though the moment she saw Cassie she jumped to her feet.

"You can't just walk in and out of my house whenever you feel like it," she said angrily. "It's one thing if we're supposed to be friends. But friends don't lie, or sneak around, or—"

"I messed up." Cassie said it simply and shrugged, letting her hands fall against her sides. "I'm so sorry. I never meant to—it all just kind of got out of control."

Greta blinked. She glanced away from Cassie for a

moment, then looked back at her, her eyes filling with tears again.

"Of all the guys in L.A. . . ." she managed to say.

"I wish you'd told me from the start," Cassie whispered. "I never would have gone near him. Not that it's your fault."

"Maybe it is," Greta said, sniffling. "I hate anyone feeling sorry for me. But maybe if I hadn't pretended I had no feelings about him in the first place . . ." She shook her head.

"I feel awful about what I did," Cassie said, almost afraid to say it, because what if Greta never forgave her? "Not just Trey." Her pulse pounded when she said his name, but she was proud of herself for not stuttering or anything. "Not just him, but lying to you. I just . . . I was so afraid of not living up to what you wanted me to be."

"What do you mean?" Greta looked bewildered. "How did I want you to be?"

"I don't know," Cassie said, shrugging helplessly. "Like you. So . . . pulled together and cool. No one ever messes with you. No one would dare. You're so . . . fearless."

Greta let out a hollow laugh. "Yeah," she said, "that's me." She rolled her eyes.

"I was so excited to be back in L.A. this summer," Cassie said. She held her hands together in front of her. "I would hate to think that I ruined everything."

"Don't be an idiot," Greta said, wiping at her nose. "Of course you didn't ruin everything. We've been friends since we were babies." She aimed a watery smile at Cassie. "I think we should blame boys. They cause all the trouble."

Cassie pictured Trey—his tender smile and the way he'd touched her face—and smiled back at Greta as best she could. She had wanted Trey as much as he had wanted her. If he *had* been playing her, she'd been more than happy to play right along.

Well, a white lie never hurt anyone, right? Not really.

"Too true," she agreed.

✦ ✦ ✦

Greta called Keagan and she came over with the contents of her parents' freezer. The three girls made their traditional gigantic sundaes and crawled out onto the roof of Greta's house to wolf them down.

"Ugh," Keagan said around a mouthful of chocolate. "I hate drama and tension and fighting. This is much better."

Greta and Cassie made assenting noises and then looked at each other quickly—almost shyly—as if to confirm it.

Cassie put her bowl aside and gazed at the view from the top of Greta's house. The red tiles were warm in the sun, and warm beneath her bare feet. To the north, she could see the Hollywood sign. It was clear enough today that she could even see the snowcapped peaks of the San Gabriel Mountains, far in the distance. Usually, the view made her feel peaceful. Today she just felt kind of sad.

Better, but sad.

"Trey was the first guy I really fell for," Greta admitted, wrapping her arms around her knees. "I mean, I *really* liked him. I was so excited when he asked me to the prom. I hardly knew what to do with myself."

Keagan sighed. "I know what that's like," she said.

"Me too," Cassie agreed. She shoved aside the part of her that hated that Greta's big story of betrayal was about Trey—*her* Trey. She had to get over it. "I won't even tell you how pathetic I was about my ex. I basically followed him around like some love-struck fool. It's really embarrassing to think about, actually." She shook off unwelcome memories of Daniel.

"And I was even more excited when we hooked up, because I thought it was the start of something," Greta said. She shook her head and then looked at Cassie. "You said I was fearless. When really I've been afraid the whole time."

"What do you have to be afraid of?" Cassie asked. "You're Greta Crocker. This city is yours." She held out her arms to encompass the whole of Los Angeles.

"Seriously," Keagan said. "I'll never forget the way you

took Zachary down in that coffee shop. It was the coolest thing I've ever seen. I would never be able to do that!"

"I've made not getting close to guys my, like, life's work," Greta said. "And on the one hand I think it's okay for girls to act like guys sometimes. Because that's only fair. But on the other hand, maybe I was just doing that because I was afraid. Because the one time I let a guy get close, he played me."

"That's a pretty good reason," Cassie said in her defense. Secretly, she couldn't help wishing it had been anyone but Trey who had done this to Greta. *Forget him,* she ordered herself. Greta was more important.

"Maybe," Greta said. "But maybe it would be better to take it on a case-by-case basis."

Keagan set her bowl next to her on the roof and wriggled her toes out in front of her like she was tickling the air.

"And maybe," she said, "kissing random boys is fun. And kind of an art. And you're an artist who needs to practice her craft."

All three of them laughed.

"I like the way you think," Greta said approvingly.

"I love you both," Keagan said gently, looking at Greta for a moment and then at Cassie. "But maybe next time you can both remember that keeping stuff all hidden and secret ended up blowing up in everyone's face."

"Yeah," Cassie said, with a rueful grin. She wished she

could reach back through the summer and change everything so no one got hurt—but she knew, somehow, that she wouldn't do it even if she could, because she couldn't bear to think about a world in which she'd never kissed Trey. She was pathetic. "We should remember that."

"I love you guys," Greta said, flopping back against the red tiles.

They all smiled at one another. And Cassie knew that whatever else might happen, this was what mattered the most. The three of them together, and happy. As it should be.

"I love you guys too," she said. "I'm going to miss you when I leave for—"

She cut herself off when both Keagan and Greta shrieked at that.

"What?" she asked, her heart thumping. "Was there an earthquake?"

"Total summer foul," Greta told her, grinning. "Never mention the end of it. What are you, crazy?"

Chapter Twenty-two

✦

At work the next week, Cassie couldn't shake her feeling that everything really had ended. She told herself it was just the simple fact that it was nearing the end of August. September was just around the corner. As she took her tours around the island, Cassie told herself she could feel a slight change in the air, in the quality of the blue sky above and the sea below.

But she suspected the change was really in her.

She did her best. She put on a happy face around her friends and tried to adhere to the summer code of never mentioning that it was coming to a close. She was thrilled that things with Greta were back on track, and that in many ways the whole blowup over Trey had brought them even closer than they'd been before. But she also knew that Greta felt that now that the air was cleared, the truth about her prom fiasco with Trey revealed, everything was good. And Cassie had to run with that, when in reality things were far from good. She ached. She thought sometimes, when she was alone in her car driving to and from the ferry stop, Missy Higgins blaring and no one to pretend for, that the sadness might permanently damage her.

As long as she kept up appearances, though, she thought she'd be fine. Eventually, she'd forget about Trey. Eventually, she'd actually feel the way she was pretending to feel. She was counting on it.

"This has been a great summer," Billy told her one morning, over one of the bike wheels he was repairing. "You really bring a nice energy to the place." He leaned back on his haunches and grinned. "Even if you do have horrible taste in music."

"Not every band can be the Grateful Dead, I know," Cassie said, rolling her eyes.

"You said it," Billy agreed with a smirk. "You'll be wearing tie-dyed shirts before you know it."

"I don't think so, but thanks," Cassie said with a big smile. And then congratulated herself for managing to fool her boss too.

"Why not take the rest of the morning to yourself?" Billy suggested. "You have a big tour this afternoon— fifteen people, I think it said."

Great. More empty hours to spend alone, trying not to burst into tears. Trying to cope with the knowledge that Trey wouldn't be appearing when she least expected it. At least when she was sitting in the shop, she had to concentrate on being normal around Billy. There was nothing to stop her from collapsing on Crescent Avenue and sobbing her heart out.

But, obviously, part of acting normal meant pretending to be delighted with a few extra hours to herself.

"Awesome!" Cassie chirped, getting to her feet. "I'll see you after lunch!"

She wandered down to one of the benches that overlooked the harbor, and very deliberately did *not* think about the night of her first real date with Trey, when they'd sat together and almost missed the ferry back to the mainland. No, she definitely wasn't thinking about that, or about the way he'd kissed her later while the ferry cut through the waves and the salt air surrounded them like a hug.

"If you were a good person," Cassie muttered to herself, "you would not have to work so hard to *not* think about someone you shouldn't be thinking about in the first place."

But she missed him. Even if she knew she was better off without him.

"He's nothing but a jerk," she told herself, and then smiled serenely at the nearby tourist couple, who raised their eyebrows and politely averted their eyes.

Terrific. Now she was scaring people.

She practically wept with joy when her phone buzzed at her, announcing an incoming message. A distraction!

HUGE END-OF-SUMMER PARTY TONIGHT IN SANTA MONICA, Greta texted. DRESS TO KILL!

Cassie stared at the text and sighed. She didn't know what she wanted to do, but she knew it did not involve any parties, huge or otherwise. She thought the last, fateful party she'd attended might actually have created a permanent aversion to summer parties. And she knew that while she could fake a certain level of being okay, she was never going to make it to a party level tonight.

U ONLY HAVE LIKE A WEEK OR 2 LEFT 2 CLAIM UR TEN-BOY-SUMMER TITLE, Keagan texted, presumably to Greta. OR TRY. I AM TOTALLY KICKING UR ASS!

IT IS ON!!! Greta texted back.

Cassie knew she was not going to be up for some Project Kiss final battle. At all. The very idea made her stomach kind of clench.

I HAVE A GIGANTIC TOUR THIS AFTERNOON ☹, Cassie texted. MIGHT BE TOO FREAKING BEAT TO DEAL. WILL KEEP U BOTH POSTED!!

She just couldn't do it. As long as she kept up her happy face, she told herself, staring out at the harbor, things would be fine. Greta and Keagan wouldn't mind if Cassie bailed, as long as she wasn't lying about stuff again. Which she wasn't.

She was annoying herself, she decided then, and got to her feet. It was high time to snap out of this funk—she just had to figure out how to do it.

A little while later, she wandered into the café and waved at Ryan as he delivered a tray of food to a table of laughing older women, all of whom seemed to want to pinch his cheeks.

"Look at you," she teased him when he came over to her. "Making time with the ladies!"

"Trolling for tips," Ryan corrected her. He flopped down into the chair across from her and grinned. "And believe me, I am good at it."

"I believe you," Cassie said with a laugh. But something must have been off about it, because Ryan frowned at her.

"You okay?" he asked.

Cassie wanted to tell him. She felt it inside of her, like a wave, but she knew that if she started she would never, ever stop. It would take her down and she wasn't sure she'd ever find a way to stop crying.

"Never better," she told him, smiling. She expected him to continue their usual banter, but Ryan was still studying her expression, that concerned frown between his eyes.

"You can tell me, Cassie," he said gently. Too kindly—it caused a lump to form in Cassie's throat.

"Really," she said. "I'm fine."

"Okay," he said, easily enough, though Cassie could see he wasn't really convinced. "Then tell me what happened with that hot stalker of yours. The one who was so deliciously Chuck Bass and didn't want to take no for an answer. I haven't seen him around in a while."

That one went straight through her heart. Cassie forced a smile.

"It's all way too boring," she said. "What about you? The last I heard, you were deciding whether or not to give your ex another chance."

Ryan sighed and rolled his eyes. "This is someone who repeatedly cheated on me, for months, with some skanky boy he met at the gym," he said. "It wasn't a *slip*. It wasn't an 'Oh my God, I was so drunk.' No. Cody and I were together for six months and he was cheating on me for five of the six months."

"Yikes," Cassie said. "You said he was evil, but you didn't tell me *how* evil!" She sat forward—thrilled to be thinking about someone else's romantic problems for a change. And at least Ryan's—unlike hers—were always entertaining.

"Because I'm over it," Ryan said with a shrug. "And I was over him too, but now suddenly he wants to come back, he tells me he's in love with me, he wants to know if I can forgive him and blah blah blah."

"I thought you were sort of seeing that other guy,"

Cassie said. "The one you met in the dog park."

"I sort of am," Ryan said. "And behold the drama that is my life—Cody knows the dog park guy. Cody took it upon himself to *call* the dog park guy and *demand* that he stay away from me!"

Cassie clapped her hands over her mouth. "He did not!" she squeaked out through her fingers.

Ryan sat back in his chair. "Oh yes," he said. "Can you believe it?"

Cassie knew that this, finally, was something she could handle. She couldn't do anything about Trey or what had happened. She couldn't seem to make herself stop longing for him, or wishing things were different. She couldn't turn back time and keep all of it from happening in the first place. All her yearning and all her sadness and all the things she felt she needed to hide beneath a smiling, happy exterior—she couldn't do a thing about any of them except wait for them to fade.

But cheating, manipulative boys who were hurting someone else? That, she could weigh in on, and with gusto.

"You need to tell him a few home truths," she told Ryan, leaning in close with the light of battle in her eyes. "He's not in charge of you—you are."

"Sing it, Cassie!" Ryan cried appreciatively.

And so she did—feeling like herself for the first time in ages.

Chapter Twenty-three

◆

can't believe it," Greta said at dinner a week later. "I can't believe it's really almost over."

"I thought that was a summer foul!" Cassie reminded her. "I'm pretty sure I almost got thrown off a rooftop for saying the exact same thing!"

"It is completely a summer foul," Greta said with a sigh, "but I can't help it."

"Tell me about it," Keagan chimed in glumly. "I've actually had to face my summer reading list, before it's too late."

The three girls looked at each other, and then out at the still-perfect summer night around them. Greta had announced that she and Keagan would be taking Cassie out to dinner in celebration of their summer—and also in recognition of the fact that Cassie was leaving for her senior year at Siskiyou in a week. Cassie had had to say goodbye to Billy, the bike shop, and to her beloved Catalina already. Billy had presented her with a collection of Grateful Dead CDs and told her the job was hers next summer if she wanted it. But Cassie couldn't think about next summer yet. There were trips to Target to plan, and new school clothes to buy, and less time, suddenly, for all the summery activities she'd been involved in since June.

California didn't make the transition easy, Cassie thought, propping her chin on her hand as she looked out at the crowd milling around the Grove, the outdoor mall at Third Street and Fairfax Avenue that felt kind of like Disneyland. The girls had commandeered a table on the outdoor patio at the Italian restaurant, and shared a pizza as they people watched. There was a fountain that leaped and shimmied to Frank Sinatra tunes, streetlamps, and even a trolley car. The summer night was no cooler than any other night; no leaves turning or early frosts to hint that the season was changing. California weather required that Cassie be on top of the reality of things, no matter how summery the night might feel.

"Here's to Project Kiss," Keagan said, lifting her drink into the air. The other two followed suit. Cassie tried to keep her expression from coming across as too rueful. After all, her summer had been less about ten boys and more about one boy who'd hit her with the impact of ten.

But she wasn't going to talk about Trey. She wasn't going to think about him, either. Too bad she had to keep reminding herself, and too bad she kept missing him so terribly.

"My total is a measly five," Cassie said, smiling as if her heart wasn't still broken from number four, and the fallout from number five.

"Five is good," Keagan said, too encouragingly, and they all laughed.

"Mine turned out to be an eleven-boy summer," Greta said, setting her drink back down and reaching for another slice. She wrinkled up her nose as she looked at Keagan. "And don't even tell me your total, you hussy!"

"Thirteen, thank you," Keagan said, and executed a mock bow in her seat.

Cassie laughed, and clapped for each of them.

"I should have known you would beat me at my own game, K," Greta said with a sigh. She licked pizza sauce off her thumb. "How about double or nothing between now and Christmas break?"

"Twenty guys?" Keagan asked. She shook her head, making her pale blond hair shimmer in the lights from the fountain. "I don't think so. I definitely had fun this summer. It was kind of liberating to just be in it for, like, a notch on my belt or whatever."

"It's totally liberating," Greta agreed.

"But I think it's better as a one-summer experiment," Keagan said. She reached over and grabbed Greta's wrist. "Don't be mad."

"Why would I be mad?" Greta propped her elbows on the table. "Really, the goal was for you not to mope about Zachary Malone all summer long."

"Mission accomplished," Keagan said fervently. She cocked her head in Cassie's direction. "What about you?"

"I definitely didn't think about Daniel," Cassie said with a laugh. Something occurred to her then, and she made a face. "I just realized I'm going to have to see him in a week. How weird will *that* be?"

"My prediction is that you won't care at all when you see him," Greta said. She waved a languid hand in the air. "He will then fall madly in love with you, and you won't even notice. Same old story every time."

Cassie allowed herself a satisfying little fantasy of Daniel begging for her time and attention, and smiled. "I kind of like that story," she said.

"I'm a little bit torn," Keagan admitted. "I was definitely into the fact that I felt I could do whatever I wanted—I want to hold on to that part." She shrugged. "But I also think I ended up making out with some guys just because they were there, and because I knew I was counting. Like they might not have made the cut if I wasn't."

"Kissing is always fun," Greta said, drawling out her declaration so that the cute guys at the next table could hear her. "No matter why you happen to be kissing someone."

Cassie thought of the guy she'd kissed at the club, when she'd called herself Delilah. It had started out fun— because it had been so novel. But then it had quickly turned awkward. Maybe that was because Delilah wasn't her. Just as Project Kiss wasn't her, exactly. She'd been living up to her idea of who Greta was—but not even Greta was that strong, fearless, untouchable person. Maybe nobody was. Maybe it was time for Cassie to be strong in her own way.

"I don't know," she said. "I want to agree with you, Greta, but I don't think I do."

"If I couldn't convince you guys after a whole summer of living it up Greta style," Greta said with a theatrical sort of sigh, "then I guess I never will. But I want you both to know I think it's totally your loss."

"We get it," Keagan said with a laugh. She looked down at her watch. "Are we going to catch that movie? Because I think it's about to start."

"We'll make it," Cassie said, basking in the pleasure of hanging out with her two oldest, best friends in the world. "And if Greta stops talking about kissing random guys for even thirty seconds, I'll buy the popcorn."

She jumped up out of her chair when Greta threw her

napkin like a homing missile, and decided that everything was perfect after all. Boys and kisses were the unimportant details. What mattered were Greta's grandiose threats, and Keagan's trademark giggle. That's what she'd take with her back to Siskiyou Academy. And long after the sad parts of the summer faded, that's what she'd remember.

Chapter Twenty-four

◆

They were all laughing so hard when Greta pulled into Cassie's driveway, as Greta reenacted a key scene from the Will Ferrell comedy they'd just seen, that it took Cassie a moment or two to register that there was someone sitting on her front steps.

And it took another heart-stopping moment to recognize that that person was Trey.

Cassie heard Greta and Keagan's laughter fade, but all she could do was drink him in with her eyes. She wanted to leap out of the car, run over, and touch him to convince herself that he was real. She wanted to hear his voice. She felt that ache that she'd had ever since they'd met spread through her.

But she'd already made her choice.

"Hey, K," she said to Keagan in the front seat, though she looked at Greta. Greta stared back, expressionless. "Could you ask him to leave?"

"Uh, sure," Keagan said. She fumbled with her seat belt.

Greta held Cassie's gaze for a long moment, but then she reached over and stopped Keagan from moving.

"Wait," she said. She lifted her shoulders as she took a breath. "You should talk to him, Cassie."

Cassie looked over and saw that Trey was walking toward the car. God, it hurt. It hurt to see him move, in that rolling, lazy way. She wished she could see his eyes, try to read his expression. He'd been so mad when she'd last seen him . . . not that it mattered now.

"Are you sure?" Cassie asked.

"Yeah," Greta said with a sigh. "Go. Talk."

Cassie squeezed her best friend's shoulder before she stood up in the backseat of the convertible and slid over the side. It took her only a few steps to be near him again. She had to take a moment to deal with their closeness. All the memories she'd been fighting so hard to keep buried since that awful night rushed back at her, almost taking her knees out from under her. That sweet, happy look on his face that night at his parents' house. The way he'd cradled her tightly to him. Cassie sucked in a breath and tried to steady herself.

"Cassie," he said, his voice soft. Exactly as it had been

when he'd once told her he loved her. The sound of it twined into her bones and weakened her resolve. But she straightened her spine. If she could turn back time, she would have avoided all of this in the first place. That's what she kept telling herself. So that's how she had to act.

"I think you should go," she said. And it cost her. It actually hurt to say the words. Cassie felt her eyes fill up with tears, but she looked away, hoping he didn't see.

"I'll go," Trey said. "I promise." He stepped around her and looked into the car, directly at Greta. "But first I want to talk to Greta."

Cassie hadn't expected that. She turned, and it was clear that Greta was just as surprised.

"What?" Greta asked. Defensively. She looked from Trey to Cassie, then back to Trey. Cassie couldn't read her expression at all. "Why?"

But Trey didn't say anything further. He waited.

Greta blew out a breath, sounding frustrated.

"Fine," she said. She climbed out of the car and slammed the driver's door with unnecessary force. "Let's talk," she snapped at Trey.

In response, he led Greta off around the side of the house, disappearing into the shadows of the backyard.

Cassie rubbed her hands over her bare arms and turned to Keagan.

"Wow," Keagan murmured, her eyes wide. She shook her head. "The plot freakin' thickens."

"Tell me about it," Cassie muttered.

And then they waited.

Keagan turned on the car and cued up Greta's iPod. One Republic started belting out "All We Are," and Cassie closed her eyes, leaned against the side of Greta's convertible, and let the late summer evening soak into her, like she had on that first night, so long ago now. She heard sirens from farther away, closer to the action of Wilshire Boulevard. She could hear the sounds of traffic on the streets around Hancock Park. She tilted her head back and looked up. There was a bright light she figured must be a satellite, and a few stars. She tried to remember the view from high up at the Observatory—all those millions of stars, crowding the sky. She tried to remind herself that from up there, her house was just one more dot of light in all the rest of the blazing lights that made up Los Angeles. Whatever happened tonight, it would still be part of the greater glow. She thought that might make the waiting easier.

After a while—it felt like days to Cassie—Trey and Greta walked back out from behind the house. Cassie straightened, studying both of them as they drew closer. Trey had his hands shoved into the pockets of his jeans, and Greta was hugging herself as she walked. As she closed the distance between them, Greta looked up, and Cassie was startled to see that she had tears in her eyes.

"Greta—" she started to say.

But Greta threw her arms around Cassie and hugged her.

"It's okay," she whispered fiercely. Her voice sounded thick. "You *should* be with him, Cassie."

"What are you talking about?" Cassie asked, confused. But she reminded herself—sharply—that it didn't matter. That she didn't need that little jump of hope in her belly that had made her heart start thumping so hard. "Listen, it doesn't matter anymore. I'm—"

"He'll explain," Greta interrupted her again. She stepped away from Cassie and looked over at Trey. It seemed like something passed between them, and then Greta turned and smiled at Cassie. "It's fine, Cassie. Really."

Cassie stood there, feeling confused and frozen, as Greta climbed back in the car. And then she and an equally confused looking Keagan drove away. Cassie had no choice but to turn and face him.

"Come on," he said, holding out his hand. "Come sit with me."

"I don't understand," Cassie said. She didn't take his hand—she knew she was way too weak for that—but she did follow him back to the front stairs. She settled herself next to him, and marveled for a moment that they were back in that same position they'd been in that first night in Catalina. Sitting so close. And yet, tonight, so far.

"I apologized to Greta," Trey said. He shifted slightly. "Something I should have done a long time ago."

"You should have told me it was her," Cassie said, not looking at him. "When I asked you about what happened. Why didn't you tell me?"

"At first I thought you knew," he said. "And then when I realized that you didn't, I didn't want to tell you. I thought . . . I knew you wouldn't be with me."

Cassie shook her head. "I guess it's good you apologized," she said. "I'm glad, for Greta's sake. She deserved it."

Trey let out a breath, and then turned so he was facing Cassie.

"I was so mad at you," he said. "I couldn't believe you were kissing that guy, and that you would actually stand there and tell me it didn't mean anything, that it was some game you had to play with your friends. Especially after the night before."

"I don't want to talk about it," Cassie said, sitting back from him. "What's the point?" She couldn't think about *the night before*—all that hope and joy at his parents' house. She already knew what it meant to her, how she held on to it. Talking about it might break her into pieces.

"Please," he said, in that quiet voice. "Please just listen."

Cassie searched his face, looking for some clue in his

dark eyes, but saw only sincerity. She nodded once, sharply, and wrapped her arms around her knees.

"But after a few days it started to dawn on me that I had that coming," Trey said. "Because before, with Greta, and other girls, I didn't care. I was this stupid jock and I liked that I was supposed to be a bad boy or something. I wanted people to think that. It wasn't personal, the things I did. I mean, it was all about me."

"I thought you already figured that out," Cassie said then. "When you had to sit out your season."

"I didn't lie to you, Cassie," he said. "I did figure some stuff out. But I didn't know what it would feel like to see a girl I was in love with do to me what I'd done to girls like Greta. I knew what I'd done was bad, but I had no idea how much it would hurt until that night."

Ah, the power to inflict pain, she thought miserably. She was the one who had not only wounded Greta, but Trey too. That must put her in the running for the worst person in the world.

"I never meant to do that to you," she managed to say.

"Cassie, stop." He reached over and put his hand on her back. She loved the feel of his warm palm against the thin fabric of her T-shirt. "I'm not blaming you."

"Maybe you should," Cassie said.

"No," he said. "This is on me. Greta told me about your pact—the ten-boy summer. Project Kiss. Believe me, it's nothing I haven't done myself."

They sat there like that for what felt like a long time. Trey's hand stayed on her back, and Cassie felt how much he meant it. He wasn't mad at her, which was good. She couldn't have lasted much longer thinking that he was off somewhere, hating her. This was better, whatever *this* was.

"You kind of took me by surprise," Trey said after a while. He smiled slightly when Cassie looked at him, that crooked smile that she loved so much. "This was supposed to be my last big summer, you know? And then you came out of nowhere at the first party I went to. *And* you were friends with a girl who hated my guts. I didn't know what to do."

"So you thought you'd just show up on my ferry," Cassie said dryly. "Interesting choice."

"I couldn't seem to stay away," Trey said. He looked at her, and there was so much feeling in his gaze that it made Cassie's heart swell and her breath catch. "I've been waiting my whole life to meet a girl like you. You're athletic and funny and really easy to hang out with. We even like the same books. You love the Observatory, and I couldn't kick your ass at bowling. You were perfectly happy to have a chili dog with me. And you're the most beautiful girl I've ever seen."

Cassie felt all the emotions she'd been fighting to hold at bay wash through her, leaving her almost dizzy. She could see how much he meant what he was saying.

She felt what she'd always felt around him—the sense that somehow, she already knew him completely. That she could see into him, and he could see into her. Like they recognized each other.

"Trey . . ." she whispered.

"I love you," he said. "I really do."

"I know," she told him, finally, the dam breaking as she leaned toward him. "I love you too."

He caught her face between his hands and kissed her, and the world tilted all around them, up and down, switching back and forth, and none of that mattered because finally, finally, she was kissing him again.

"I leave for school in a week," she told him, pulling away.

"So do I," Trey said, pulling her close again and laying soft kisses along her cheek, her jaw. "Why don't we just enjoy the last few days of summer while we can?" He looked at her. "Without sneaking around."

Cassie felt her smile start deep inside and spread upward, until she could feel herself beaming at him.

"That sounds perfect," she said.

Trey kissed her again, and then pulled her closer, across his lap, so he could hold her tight to him. Cassie felt like screaming her happiness to the world, but decided her parents and the neighbors would probably appreciate if she kept it to herself. She could feel her skin practically hum with it.

"So . . ." Trey said, looking down at her, as he toyed with the front of her hair. "About this ten-boy summer." His eyebrows crept up his forehead. "Exactly how well did you do?"

Cassie let out some of that happiness in her laughter, and then allowed herself a one hundred percent Greta smile.

"Wouldn't you like to know?" she teased him.

It might not have been the summer she'd planned, or thought she wanted, but Cassie couldn't think of a better ending.

What happens when Celeste's jealous
boyfriend meets her flirtatious ex-fling? Read
on for a peek of Hailey Abbott's

FLIRTING WITH BOYS

✦

After spending the day graduation party-hopping,
Travis drove his purring BMW up to the darkened
entrance of Pinyon. Two spotlights illuminated the
sandstone sign as Devon hopped out of the backseat.

"I'll give you kids a minute to say good night. See
you up at the house, Celeste." Devon pranced up the
drive barefoot, dangling her shoes in her hand.

Celeste could just make out Travis's face. His dark
eyes seemed huge. The lights from the dashboard illuminated his high, flat cheekbones. She leaned over the
gearshift and pressed herself against him. A wave of
warmth spread over her body as he pushed his hand
under the hair at the back of her neck. She closed her
eyes and felt his lips press against hers.

"I'm so glad you're working here this summer," she murmured.

"If the whole summer's going to be like this, I am too." His voice rasped in the darkness.

"Call me tomorrow?"

"Of course," he said, pulling her toward him for one last kiss.

Celeste waved to him from the entrance. The sleek metal gate slid shut behind her as she turned up the path toward the main building. She pushed through the fence that surrounded the pool area and followed the stone path around a clump of tall cypresses to the staff quarters, which included her parents' house. Celeste had lived in the little gray-painted bungalow since she was four years old, when her parents bought the resort.

Celeste spotted her best friend Devon by the front door and held her finger to her lips. She eased the door open and the girls crossed the front hall and tiptoed to Celeste's bedroom, where Devon dove under the comforter. "Mmm, it's so nice and warm in here." She closed her eyes and pulled the blanket up.

As Celeste stepped over Devon's discarded pink platforms, she noticed a piece of paper under them. She picked it up and groaned internally when she recognized her father's handwriting. The usual morning instructions. Dad must have pushed it under her door earlier in the evening. "Goodbye, carefree summer," she muttered to herself as she opened the sheet of scrap paper.

Celeste sat on the edge of the bed. "Move over," she said to Devon, who was already making little snoring noises.

"Mmmmm," her friend replied. She moved her leg a half-inch to the right.

Celeste lay back and scanned the note. *Celeste Tippen and Devon Wright: Instructions for Monday, June 20,* the heading said. Her dad had such a warm and fuzzy way about him. She read on. *Celeste: (1) Check and refill all towel stations with new Ralph Lauren towels. (2) Prep all cabanas: Evian spritzer bottles, water pitchers, Kiehl's sunscreen samples. (3) Prep for Saunders family arrival: check guesthouse, deliver fruit basket, greet car 10:30 a.m.*

Celeste bolted upright on the bed and let out a strangled squeak, like a mouse that had been stepped on. The note fluttered out of her limp hand onto the floor. "Devon!" she croaked in a strangled voice. "Devon, wake up! I'm in huge, giant trouble!"

"Mmmrrr?" Devon pushed open one eyelid. "What is it?" she muttered.

Celeste shook her friend. "This is a major crisis!"

Devon rolled over onto her stomach. "Is it a major crisis that can wait until morning?"

"Nick Saunders!" Celeste stage-whispered.

"Who?" Devon peeked at Celeste with one eye.

"Nick Saunders! Remember, that guy who stays here every summer?"

"Kind of. Is he the one who's always bugging you to get him things?"

"Yeah, that's him. His family's from L.A.—his dad is some sort of big-time movie producer or something. Anyway, they're filthy rich and Nick totally knows it. He's always asking me to, like, get him this one special cheese sandwich from a place twenty-five miles away, and make sure it's on only white bread, extra mayonnaise—stuff like that."

"Riiiiight . . . I remember him now," Devon said. She propped herself up on her elbows. "Wait, hang on, didn't something happen with you and him last summer?"

Celeste closed her eyes and put a pillow over her face. "Yes."

"What? I can't hear you," Devon said. "Your voice is all muffly."

Celeste lowered the pillow slightly. "I said yes. We've always been super-flirty with each other, and last summer we kinda hooked up. A few times. Okay, lots of times."

"You bad girl!"

"I wasn't bad! Travis and I had barely started dating. And it was *his* idea not to be exclusive while we spent the summer apart."

"Well, what did Travis say about Nick?"

"Umm." Celeste paused. She was glad for the pillow on her face, because she could feel her cheeks flaming. "Actually, I didn't tell him. It was just a dumb flirtation followed by a convenient summer fling. But now they're

4

destined to meet! If Nick is even one-third as obnoxious as usual, Travis is going to freak out. You know how jealous he can get."

"So does Nick, like, *like* you or something?" Devon asked.

Celeste snorted. She rolled onto her stomach and gazed out the window at her view of the storage shed. "Hah, no. He's just totally bored stuck out here in the desert. He needs a target for his flirting and I just happen to be here. But I'm not sure I trust Travis to look past the 'I used to make out with your girlfriend' part of the situation."

Devon flopped back down and closed her eyes again. "Oh, don't worry about it. I'll be there to make sure everyone behaves themselves." She grinned.

"Yeah, sure—Devon Wright, moral guardian. Can't wait to see what your nun's cape looks like."

"Oh my God, that's brilliant," Devon mumbled. "That's my next Halloween costume—slutty nun."

"Good night, Dev."

Celeste heaved herself up from the bed. In her minuscule bathroom, she gazed at her reflection in the mirror. Wide brown eyes and a worried frown stared back at her. Despite Devon's reassurance, if today was any indication of the emotional roller coaster she was going to ride this summer, there was a good chance not everyone would make it out alive.

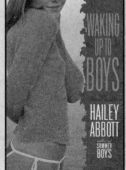

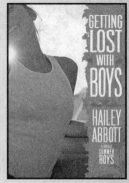